The Secret of the Oak Tree

The air is perfectly still. No leaves rustle. No bird sings. Penny is utterly alone. She has learned the secret of the ancient Druid oak and has come to destroy it.

"Don't let me fail," she prays.

Suddenly the bare branches of the tree are writhing like masses of huge snakes... reaching out for her.

Other Avon Camelot Books by
Lou Kassem

A HAUNTING IN WILLIAMSBURG
MIDDLE SCHOOL BLUES
THE TREASURES OF WITCH HAT MOUNTAIN

Avon Flare Books
LISTEN FOR RACHEL

LOU KASSEM is the author of a number of books for young people including *Listen for Rachel* and *Middle School Blues,* also available from Avon Books. She lives in Blacksburg, Virginia, and when she's not writing, she's trying to master the game of golf.

Avon Books are available at special quantity discounts for bulk purchases for sales promotions, premiums, fund raising or educational use. Special books, or book excerpts, can also be created to fit specific needs.

For details write or telephone the office of the Director of Special Markets, Avon Books, Dept. FP, 1350 Avenue of the Americas, New York, New York 10019, 1-800-238-0658.

THE DRUID CURSE

LOU KASSEM

AN AVON CAMELOT BOOK

If you purchased this book without a cover, you should be aware that this book is stolen property. It was reported as "unsold and destroyed" to the publisher, and neither the author nor the publisher has received any payment for this "stripped book."

THE DRUID CURSE is an original publication of Avon Books. This work has never before appeared in book form.

AVON BOOKS
A division of
The Hearst Corporation
1350 Avenue of the Americas
New York, New York 10019

Copyright © 1994 by Lou Kassem
Published by arrangement with the author
Library of Congress Catalog Card Number: 94-94464
ISBN: 0-380-77593-X
RL: 5.0

All rights reserved, which includes the right to reproduce this book or portions thereof in any form whatsoever except as provided by the U.S. Copyright Law. For information address Ruth Cohen, Inc., Literary Agency, P.O. Box 7626, Menlo Park, California 94025.

First Avon Camelot Books Printing: November 1994

CAMELOT TRADEMARK REG. U.S. PAT. OFF. AND IN OTHER COUNTRIES, MARCA REGISTRADA, HECHO EN U.S.A.

Printed in the U.S.A.

OPM 10 9 8 7 6 5 4 3 2 1

For Gwen Montgomery:
editor extraordinaire, my tenth muse

Foreword

Once long ago in Celtic Britain a religious sect called Druidism flourished. Druids kept no written records.

Julius Caesar described the character and functions of the Druids. "They attend to divine worship, perform public and private human sacrifices, and expound matters of religion. A great number of youths are gathered around them for the sake of education.

"The Druids take no part in warfare. Beyond all things, they are desirous to inspire a belief that men's souls do not perish but transmigrate after death from one individual to another living thing. They are wizards and magicians of great renown. The Druids hold the oak tree and mistletoe as sacred."

With the advance of the Roman legions and the spread of Christianity, the Druids were driven out of Britain . . . or at least into secrecy.

Kidwelly, Wales, October 31, 1675

"Tonight! Two bells after Evensong. Come prepared."

The bent farmer acknowledged the miller's whispered message with a curt nod, picked up the grain sack, and trudged away.

The farmer and the miller were not the only ones passing secrets. The entire village of Kidwelly buzzed like a hive of bees. Perhaps it could be explained by the date— All Hallows' eve. In spite of their professed Christianity, the villagers were superstitious and believed evil spirits roved about on the night before All Saints' Day. Parents kept their children close to the hearth this night. In fact, very few adults ventured forth on All Hallows' eve. Tonight was different. As the harvest moon rose in the clear October sky, shadowy figures began to converge on the village church. Grim, determined men armed with bows, axes, knives, and cudgels gathered silently in the churchyard.

A black-robed priest emerged from the church and stood before the armed, silent villagers. Father Stephen spoke with a quiet intensity. "This abomination must be removed from us! Our Lord can no longer tolerate these pagan practices. Human sacrifices to a pagan god is an offense punishable by eternal damnation. The Druids have been warned and called to repent. They have not done so. Instead, they practice their unholy religion in secret. But the Lord has shown us the way through his servant, Selwyn ap Cryn. Selwyn has found their secret meeting place." The priest paused, then let his voice ring out in command. "Tonight the army of the Lord shall destroy these Druids and their cursed tree!"

"Amen!" responded the crowd.

With only the moon for light, the armed band moved silently into the Cambrian forest. The moon had reached its zenith when the villagers arrived at a clearing. Long before they could see anything, they could hear a sonorous chanting that built in intensity every moment.

On Father Stephen's signal, the villagers swiftly and silently encircled the clearing.

Inside the clearing, fifty or more men and women were gathered, facing a giant oak tree. At the base of the oak stood a white-robed old man. A crown of oak leaves sat upon his snowy hair. In his left hand he held a wreath of mistletoe. In his right hand a dagger gleamed. A rough stone slab formed an altar at his feet. Three small fires ringed the altar.

The chanting ceased.

The old man waved the mistletoe over the fire. Flames shot skyward, revealing a young girl lying on the altar looking up expectantly at the Druid priest.

"Stop, in the name of the Lord!" shouted Father Stephen.

For a split second, no one moved.

Then the Druid priest's right hand flashed down. Bright red blood spurted upward like water from a fountain.

One of the attacking villagers screamed in anguish. "My daughter! My Gwynn! He killed my Gwynn!"

At his cry the villagers attacked the unarmed worshipers.

The Druid priest did not move. He stood imperiously behind the altar, his white robe now spattered with blood. Suddenly his voice rang out, deep and authoritative, like thunder, in a language the villagers could not understand. As he spoke, the other Druids ceased their struggles. Eyes flashing with fanatical fire, the priest turned to Father Stephen and spat some unintelligible words. Then he whirled and embraced the giant oak.

One of the villagers thought the priest was escaping and shot an arrow into his back.

The Druid priest was impaled upon the oak.

"Enough!" Father Stephen cried. "Selwyn, gather some men and chop down this abomination. We must burn every scrap of it."

Everyone hastened to obey.

Later, as Selwyn and his men chopped at the massive tree, the miller asked, "What said the old Druid, Selwyn?"

Selwyn's face was red and sweaty from his efforts. Now a look of fear came into his eyes. "I know not," he muttered.

"It was ancient Celtic, was it not?"

"Aye, mayhap it was."

"You being a traveler, you understand the old tongue, do you not?"

Seeing that the miller was not going to let it go, Selwyn nodded glumly. "Aye, it was the bard's tongue. A curse, near as I could fathom. Some nonsense about his soul and the oak being one and living forever. I couldn't make out all of it."

"Did he curse us or just Father Stephen?"

Selwyn was becoming more frightened as they talked.

"Leave off, man! Let's get on with this tree. I'm for home and bed before dawn."

Dawn came and the task was not complete. Green wood burns slowly. One by one the villagers drifted away.

Father Stephen ran after the last ones. "Come back! Every twig must be burned," he cried. But despite his pleading, no one wanted to go back to the cursed glen.

"I'll finish the job for you ... for a sum," offered a stranger who was coming along the road. "Name's Ian Cooper. Just passing through on my way to Bristol and the New World. Short of funds. I don't fear these Druids."

Father Stephen had no choice. He gave Ian Cooper a sum of money and directions to the glen. "You're to stay nearby until all the fires are out. We don't wish the whole of the Cambrian forest burnt."

"Aye, I'll do the job right, Father," promised Ian.

A pair of curious eyes watched Ian work. Well hidden in the deep brush, Padric Moore observed the man's actions.

Padric was twelve, and like most children, curious. He had seen the struggle of villagers coming from the wood and heard Father Stephen ranting at them. He wondered what had taken place on All Hallows' eve, so he followed the stranger and observed the burning of the huge oak. He felt the ominous, brooding silence of the glen and was afraid. Yet he stayed to watch.

Toward evening, Padric saw the man wrap two pieces of the oak tree in a blanket and pack them on his sturdy pony. Whistling, the man started off on the track toward Bristol.

"Now that's passing strange," mused Padric. "Not only does he begin his journey at the end o' day, but he hides the wood he set aside." Now that the man had departed, the silence in the glen was absolute.... Not a birdsong, leaf rustle, or insect chirp broke the stillness. Sweat broke out on Padric's brow. He rose from his hiding place on shaky legs and began running, vowing he would never visit the glen again or tell anyone of his shameful fear.

Years passed. Father Stephen still ministered to the villagers of Kidwelly. He was a good priest, but he still saw Druids behind every rock and tree. He did not believe, as the villagers did, that the Druids had been done away with on that terrible night long ago.

Padric Moore grew up strong, handsome, and still adventurous. He was the third son of Gwolf Moore and had very dim prospects of inheriting any of his father's land. Padric decided to seek his fortune in the New World. The day before he was to depart, he sought Father Stephen's blessing on his journey. Though he could see no reason for it, he told Father Stephen of his youthful spying adventure.

Father Stephen listened in silence, with a look of growing horror on his face. He made Padric repeat the story twice.

"Father, I'm sorry I upset you. I was only a lad," Padric said. "Bless my journey and I'll be on my way."

Father Stephen's face was the color of yesterday's ashes. "No, my son, I cannot bless you now. I must have time.... Come back in two days."

"I will, Father," Padric said, humoring the old priest. He did not intend to delay his trip.

The priest's eyes flashed. "Do not lie to me, Padric Moore. You have been given a task by our Lord. Refuse to do it and you will be eternally damned."

A nervous Padric Moore returned two days later.

"You'd best be told the whole story," Father Stephen said with a sigh. He proceeded to tell Padric what had transpired on All Hallows' eve ten years past. "Evil does exist in the world, Padric. We did not stamp it out, no matter what the villagers think. The wood of that oak was cursed. Only burning ends the curse. Now you come and tell me it was not all burned.''

"Only a few pieces escaped the fire, Father."

"One piece is enough!"

Padric shuddered, remembering the fear he'd felt in the glen. "But, Father, that was ten years ago. What has that to do with me now?"

Looking Padric straight in the eye, Father Stephen replied, "You were sent to the glen for a purpose, Padric. You may think you went out of curiosity. We don't always understand the ways of our Lord. The power of evil exists. But so does the power of good. You were sent to watch and see that no evil tricks were played. Well, you saw and your fear made you keep silent. Until now. You have failed in the task the Lord gave you, Padric. And by failing you have let loose the Druid's curse on innocent souls."

"What must I do?"

"You must find Ian Cooper. Find out what he did with the wood he took unlawfully."

"After ten years? And him on his way to the New World?"

Father Stephen's eyes burned into Padric's with the intensity of hot coals. "You must, Padric! That is your mission, even if it takes a lifetime. Find that man and the Druid oak. When you find it, destroy it!"

"Where do I start, Father?"

"At Bristol. Inquire after Ian Cooper there. Go where the trail leads you. And, Padric, keep a record of your quest. Send it back to me or pass it on to your sons. Never rest until you have destroyed the Druid oak! It may not be as hard as you think. Evil leaves a trail, much as a wounded animal leaves a trail of blood."

Padric knelt. "Bless me, Father. Pray I find the courage and strength to do what is asked of me."

Father Stephen removed a cross from his neck. It was a simple cross carved from stone, worn smooth with years of loving touches. He slipped it over Padric's bowed head. "Wear this in your search, my son. It will offer some measure of protection." Then, taking a scroll from under his robe, he bent and whispered into Padric's ear, "The means of the Druid oak's destruction is written here. Magic to like magic. Go with God."

Thus, on an April day in 1685, Padric Moore left his home and began the search for Ian Cooper.

Massachusetts Colony, 1740

"Prudence, where have you been?"

The angular woman stood in the cabin doorway and looked sternly at the little girl standing, head down, in the yard. Both females were dressed alike in dull butternut homespun dresses, white aprons, and white caps.

"Has the cat gotten your tongue, Prudence?" The woman's voice carried a hint of laughter.

Hearing this sign of relenting wrath, the child looked up and smiled. "Nay, Mother. I still have my tongue ... and something else," she said, bringing from behind her back a bucket filled with nuts. "See, I brought a whole bucketful for you."

The woman took the proffered nuts but kept her voice stern. "You were told to stay with your brother. Jonathan came home long ago! He said you wandered off again."

Prudence frowned. "Jonathan walks too fast. I couldn't keep up. I went to my secret place for the nuts. It wasn't far off Salem Road, Mother. I thought you'd be pleased."

"Prudence Miller, you are surely a worry!" Dame Miller scolded. "You have been told time and time again not to wander. The Indians and wild beasts are a danger to us all. You must learn to stop and think before you act so hastily."

"I will remember next time, Mother," Prudence promised contritely.

"Come inside and help me prepare the evening meal, then. Perhaps we will roast some of your chinquapins tonight."

While helping her mother, Prudence chattered like a blue jay. The drab clothes and humble cabin could not suppress the sparkle and gaiety of the little girl.

Dame Miller listened with half an ear as she bustled around the room that served for both eating and cooking.

"Don't you think that's strange?"

Prudence's question startled Dame Miller. "What? What is strange?"

"You weren't listening, Mother," Prudence chided.

"Nay, I was woolgathering, I suppose. What was strange?"

"The tree. I was telling you about my secret place where this big oak tree suddenly appeared."

"Prudence, trees don't suddenly appear! It takes years to grow a tree. You know that."

"This tree wasn't there last autumn," insisted Prudence. "It came to my secret place during the winter."

Dame Miller looked carefully at her daughter. "Do you have a fever, Prue? Do you need some tonic?"

"No, Mother, I feel fine," Prudence said quickly. "Perhaps I was mistaken. Perhaps I didn't look carefully last year."

Dame Miller smiled. "You must show me your wondrous place someday."

"Oh, you'd like my secret place, Mother. It's beautiful. Can we go tomorrow?"

"Perhaps. If not tomorrow, soon."

Dame Miller never saw her daughter's secret place or her magical tree.

On that same evening, October 31, while making a visit to the privy, Prudence vanished.

It was believed she had been taken by the Indians.

Catskill Mountains, New York, 1875

" 'Tis going to be a fine day! The sun will burn off the mist before we leave."

"Sally, come away from that window! Finish dressing. Mama needs me to dish breakfast."

"Aren't you just a tiny bit excited, Mary?" Sally asked as she closed the shutters. "Harvest festival day! A whole day in the village!" She twirled around in her second-best homespun blue dress.

Mary, being almost three years older than Sally, tried to suppress her own rising excitement as befitted a grown girl of fourteen. "Of course, I'm excited, Sally. This year I get to stay for the barn dance. Now, hold still while I braid this curly hair of yours!"

On Sally's lips a pout formed. "I wish I could go to the barn dance. Julie Stewart is going and she's my age."

"Your turn will come. Papa let me go last year with Uncle Josh."

"I don't care about dancing. I want to ride home in the hay wagon with my friends and sing songs in the moonlight!" exclaimed Sally.

Mary giggled in anticipation. "I'll tell you all about it," she promised. "There! Your hair's all done."

"Mary! Sally! Hurry on down. Your papa and brothers will be in soon for breakfast," Mrs. Hungate called from below.

After breakfast, the Hungates loaded their wagon for the three-mile trip to Cableskill. The sun burned through the autumn mist just as Sally had predicted. The air was crisp and the sky a brilliant blue. A perfect day, this last day of October, for the harvest festival.

Cableskill was a sleepy little village of about fifty inhabitants. But at harvest festival the number swelled to two hundred or more. Farm families from miles around brought the best of their stock, comestibles, and handcrafts to be judged. After all the prizes were awarded, most of the farmers gathered their tired families and headed home for the evening chores.

Young people, of the proper age, stayed on for the traditional harvest dance at Hutton's barn. It was the last social event of the year until Christmas.

Mary Hungate was a budding beauty with cornsilk blond hair, violet eyes, and rosy lips that always seemed turned up in a smile. She danced almost every dance this year, including four dances with Jason Walters. A fact duly noted by the older folk who were chaperoning.

At eleven o'clock everyone piled into the waiting hay wagons to be driven home. Mary climbed into the wagon driven by her uncle Josh. Jason Walters climbed in beside her. "Mind if I sit with you, Mary?" he asked timidly.

"Plenty of room, Jason," Mary replied, sliding over.

The wagon was soon filled with laughing young people. "Everyone in that's going out on the river road?" Josh Hungate called out.

"Everyone's here, Mr. Hungate. Don't go too fast though. Don't want to tire those fine horses," someone answered.

A huge golden moon sailed in the black, star-filled sky as the horses moved off at a slow pace. Someone started a song and everyone joined in. Later, Thomas Engle started telling a ghost story. This gave the young couples a reason to huddle closer together in the sweet, fresh hay.

Occasionally, the wagon would stop and some unlucky person who lived close to town would have to get out and go home. At midnight the wagon reached the tree-lined lane that led to the Hungate farm. Josh Hungate stopped the wagon. "Your place, Mary," he called out.

"I'll go with you," Jason offered as Mary jumped down.

"Never mind, Jason," Mary said, pleased. "It isn't far."

"I can't wait for you, Jason," Josh said. "I have to be up for chores before the cock crows."

Mary waved good-bye and watched as the wagon disappeared around the bend. Someone had begun another song. She pulled her woolen shawl closer and started up the lane. What a grand day! I wish we had harvest festival several times a year, she thought. Last year I only danced a few dances. This year I danced almost every one. Four with Jason! She giggled with delight. I can hardly wait to tell Sally all about it. Well, maybe not *all,* she thought, remembering the stolen kisses.

A chill wind blew some clouds over the moon. Suddenly the lane was very dark and unfamiliar.

Mary was picking her way carefully along the wagon ruts, but she increased her pace. A shiver ran down her spine. She clutched her shawl tighter. "Don't be a silly goose!" she told herself. "A girl with a new beau is too grown-up to be afraid of the dark. It's only Tommy Engle's ghost story that has you all goose-pimpley."

Somehow she wasn't comforted by her brave words.

Her heart began to flutter against her ribs like a trapped bird. She could hear it saying *run—run—run—RUN*.

Mary ran.

Something big and dark loomed in her path. Was it a tree?

"I must have wandered out of the lane," Mary whispered. "I know there's no tree here."

Before she could cry out, writhing limbs enveloped her, squeezing, slashing, tearing. . . .

Mary Hungate was never seen again. No trace of her was ever found.

In the town of Cableskill, nestled on the banks of the Susquehanna River, Mary Hungate is still remembered. Her story is the favorite mystery tale told every Halloween.

Maryland, October 31, 1951

The engine sputtered, coughed, and finally ground to a halt.

Katy Sullivan steered the coasting car as far off the country road as possible. "Darn and double darn!" she said as the car came to a shuddering stop. She looked at the needle on the gas gauge. It sat stubbornly on quarter-tank mark, as it had for the last twenty or thirty miles. "Well, Bob said the darned thing was off! He didn't say by how much though. I should have filled up back in Westminster."

Drumming her fingers on the steering wheel, Katy tried to decide what to do. She had left Baltimore after the dinner meal at Goucher College. By taking all of Bob's recommended shortcuts, she should have arrived at St. Joseph's College in Emmitsburg by eleven o'clock. Plenty of time for a good night's sleep before tomorrow's festivities and the big harvest ball Saturday night. Now she was stuck in the middle of nowhere! Sighing, she turned off her lights. "No use having a dead battery, too."

The darkness was absolute. Not one glimmer of light showed anywhere. "I guess country people go to bed early even on Halloween," she said, climbing out of the car and locking it.

A sharp wind cut through her jacket. "*Br-r-r!* Bet there weren't many trick-or-treaters out tonight." Stuffing her hands in her pockets, she trudged off.

A short while later, as she crested a hill, she saw lights in the distance. "Ah, civilization!"

Just ahead, a figure in white stepped from the adjoining woods and held up a hand in greeting.

"Hi," Katy called, returning the wave. "My car broke down. Could you—"

Something coiled around her neck, lifting her high into the black night....

Katy Sullivan's locked, abandoned car was found on November 1, 1951.

CHAPTER ONE

Blue Ridge Mountains, Virginia—the present

A low growl rumbled from the German shepherd's throat. His hackles stood stiff and straight.

Penny looked up from her sketch pad, tossing back her long chestnut hair. "Hush, Rusty. I know we've been here a while, but I can't seem to get this little glen right."

Standing, ears erect, Rusty growled again.

"All right. Go chase your squirrel or whatever."

Instead of bounding happily away, Rusty moved closer to her, baring his teeth and glaring down into the peaceful glen.

Penny put her hand on his back. "Easy, boy. No wild animal I know of makes that much racket." Under her hand she felt the dog quiver. Then his head swung toward the slope on her right. The noise grew louder. Penny laughed. "Your hearing's great but your sense of direction needs work, boy."

Seconds later a mop of curly black hair atop a dirt-streaked face popped through a tangle of rhododendron. Panic mixed with surprise showed clearly on the boy's face. Keeping his blue eyes fixed on her, he battled the dense branches until all six feet of him emerged. "Are you for real or a mirage?" he asked shakily.

"Real," Penny answered, biting her lip to keep from smiling at the scraggly stranger.

Rusty wagged his tail.

"Right. Guess mirages only happen in the desert. Uh— do you know where I am? I've been wandering in these woods for hours."

"You're on Little Bear Mountain in the Virginia Blue Ridge."

"Hey, at least I'm in the right state," he said with a forced smile. "Am I close to the parkway? Anywhere near the community of Glyn Ayr?"

"It's about two miles to Glyn Ayr and about a mile to the parkway . . . as the crow flies."

Panic returned to his eyes. "In which direction?"

"I'll lead you out," Penny said, swallowing a small sigh. This wasn't her first lost hiker. Sometimes people didn't respect her mountains. She carefully slipped her sketch pad into her backpack and stood. "Which one? The parkway or Glyn Ayr?"

"Whichever's easier," he said, thrusting out a big, long-fingered hand. "I'm Christopher Williams. Just moved to Glyn Ayr last month. From Alexandria. Guess I haven't gotten my mountain legs yet."

Surprised, she put her small hand in his. "Penelope Brown." Then she glanced at his pale legs decorated with briar scratches. "You should wear long pants hiking."

"I didn't *intend* to go hiking. See, I saw this whole mass of *Danaus plexipi* and started following them. First thing I knew, they were gone and I was lost."

"Uh-huh." She had no idea what this city slicker meant and wasn't about to ask. "Let's go." She started off with the boy following close at her heels.

Neither of them saw the figure that rose from the underbrush down in the glen and glared after them with a mixture of surprise, hatred, and cunning.

The boy chattered a mile a minute. "Mom and I have only been here two weeks. We inherited Uncle Pat's place. Everyone calls it the Wilcox house. You know it?"

"Sure. Big brick on River Road."

"That's the one. After having it remodeled and all, Uncle Pat didn't get to enjoy it."

Penny glanced back in surprise. "Was your uncle the professor who fell down Little River Gorge?"

"Yeah. Ex-professor, actually. He'd resigned from the University of Virginia a few years before he died."

"I didn't know he had passed away."

"He lived a couple of months after the accident," the boy replied shortly. "You live in Glyn Ayr, Penelope?"

"No, I live out from town. In Fox Hollow." She hesitated, then said, "Everyone calls me Penny."

"Too bad. You look more like a Penelope."

"Oh? How's a Penelope supposed to look?"

The boy chuckled. "Mythical, magical. Just like you sitting on that rock. You could have stepped right out of Greek mythology."

"Well, I'm not Greek. And folks call me Penny."

He wasn't flustered by her sharp tone. "Yeah, people do shorten names, don't they? Everyone calls me Chris. Except Mom when she's mad. Then I'm Christopher Patrick Williams."

Penny smiled to herself. City folks and country folks had something in common. "Speaking of names, what's this *Danaus plexipi* you were chasing?"

"Monarch butterflies. I never saw so many at one time. Awesome!"

"They come every year," Penny said. "They're migrating to their winter home."

"It's totally awesome!"

When they reached a trail Chris pulled up beside her. His breathing was a little ragged, but he didn't complain about the fast pace. "You know, I read three books on hiking ... two on the Blue Ridge Mountains.... Nothing prepared me for these woods. How do you know where you're going?"

Penny paused to let him catch his breath. "I grew up here. I know these woods like the back of my hand."

Chris's eyes darted nervously to the tall trees surrounding them. "I don't think I'll ever get the hang of it. One tree looks pretty much like another to me."

"I reckon I'd get lost in the city."

"No, you wouldn't," Chris said, laughing. "Cities have street signs."

Penny looked away. Street signs wouldn't help if you had trouble reading them. "Trees aren't all the same," she mumbled. "Not if you take time to look."

"I'll bet you take the time. I saw your sketchbook. You an artist?"

"I want to be," Penny replied, feeling the heat rise in her face.

"That's neat! I can't draw a straight line with a ruler."

In spite of herself, she giggled. "Artists don't use rulers."

It was Chris's turn to blush. "Yeah. Right."

"I'm not a real artist or anything," Penny added hastily. "I just like to draw and paint what I see around me."

"Hey, don't put yourself down. I bet you're good. Besides, isn't that what an artist does? Paint what she sees, I mean."

"I guess." Penny began walking again. Chris made her

uncomfortable. She was much more at ease around adults than people her own age. Especially boys.

In a few long strides, Chris caught up. "Guess getting lost won't do my local rep any good. I mean, if anyone should find out . . ."

Penny gave him a disgusted look. "I don't tell tales out of school."

A sheepish grin played over Chris's face. "Thanks, Penny. It's tough enough moving to a new place without everyone thinking you're a major klutz."

Penny nodded. She understood his feelings if not his words. He sure did talk funny.

"Speaking of school," Chris continued, "I'll be a freshman at Wayne County High. What year are you?"

Penny's lips tightened. "I'm in eighth grade. Why?"

"Just thought I'd found a classmate," Chris said with a lopsided grin. "I hate moving into a new school and not knowing anybody. It's the pits! A friendly face on the first day makes all the difference."

He's like a big, friendly puppy, Penny thought. I can't imagine him ever having trouble making friends. She stopped abruptly and pointed. "There's the road. Glyn Ayr's just around that big curve. You can't miss it." While he was looking where she'd pointed, Penny melted into the trees.

"Hey, Penny! Come back. . . ."

Penny kept going until she could no longer hear his voice. He wouldn't follow her. He was too afraid of the woods. Feeling a little guilty, she circled around and waited until she could see the road and Chris loping along it. "Okay, Rusty. The greenhorn's safe. Let's get on home."

The dog licked her hand and bounded off through the trees.

Sighing, Penny ambled down one trail and up another without paying much attention to where she was going. Her feet knew the way. She had other things to think about besides lost boys. Like going over to the Waysider tomorrow. Aunt Martha had practically promised Miz Hawkins Penny would take the job. Aunt Martha said it would be good for her.

Maybe.

But Penny dreaded losing any of her precious weekends—five days lost in school was bad enough. Even the prospect of having some money of her very own didn't make up for it.

She sat down with her back against a tree and pulled out her pad and charcoal. With a few deft strokes, she captured Chris Williams's face. "He has good bones," she murmured. "He'll grow into that lanky frame and make a right handsome man one day."

Her words made her blush. What did she care how an older Chris would look? Once he found out about Penny Brown he wouldn't give her the time of day. Sighing, she put away her things and whistled for Rusty.

Rusty dashed from the woods and together they proceeded up Fox Hollow past the heavy-laden apple trees marching in neat, wide columns up and down the 128 acres of the MacAfee orchards. Already the air had a faint winey scent. The heady aroma would deepen in September and October as windfall apples perfumed the air.

"We're gonna have a good crop this year, Rusty," she said, taking a deep breath of the fragrant air.

As they neared the sprawling old farmhouse, Penny saw a brown car parked out front and Aunt Martha standing on the porch, shading her eyes for a better view of the road.

"Hurry along, Penny," Aunt Martha called, waving her in. "Someone's here to see you."

Penny recognized the county sheriff's car as she got closer. "Oh, Rusty! Have you been chasing the Parkers' chickens again?"

Rusty looked at her with a "who me?" expression.

"Don't give me that innocent look! Deputy Coombs only comes out here when you've been bad or to buy apples. It's too early for apples. That leaves *you*. Aren't you ashamed?"

For an answer, Rusty calmly lifted his leg and sprayed the sheriff's tires.

"Bad dog," she said, giggling. She was still laughing when she went inside.

Sheriff Vince Peale wasn't laughing. His face looked as if he'd bitten into a lemon. Aunt Martha and Uncle Jake looked solemn, too.

Penny's heartbeat quickened. "What's Rusty done now?"

"I'm not here about your dog. I'm here about a murder."

CHAPTER TWO

"Murder? Who's been murdered?" Penny asked, looking from her somber aunt and uncle back to Sheriff Peale.

The sheriff fixed her with a flinty stare. "Please sit down, Penny."

Obediently, she sat in a chair opposite her uncle and aunt.

The sheriff remained standing. "You heard about the body found by those two city boys hiking on Big Bear Mountain?"

Penny nodded. "We saw it on the news. Do you know who it was now, Sheriff?"

Unlike Deputy Coombs, who was laid-back and slightly rumpled, Sheriff Peale was a spit-and-polish ex-Marine. His manner was as sharp as the creases in his trousers. "We have a positive identification. Melissa Burke. You remember her?"

"Yes," Penny answered. Everyone in Wayne County had cause to remember the girl in Penny's class who'd disappeared into thin air last October. Police, fire, and rescue squads, park rangers, and volunteers had searched for days without finding a trace of Melissa. "What was she doing on Big Bear?"

"That's what we'd like to know," the sheriff snapped. "So far, no one in this entire county admits to ever having been up there."

"There's a reason for that," Jake said. "That limestone mountain's dangerous. Full of caves and sinkholes. Even the Indians knew it was bad medicine. Locals avoid it."

"I'm aware of the local superstitions, Mr. MacAfee," Sheriff Peale said. "However, some people *do* go up there. Right, Miss Brown?"

Martha shook her head emphatically. "No, Sheriff. That's one place Penny's been told not to go."

Penny couldn't stop the flush that rose to her face.

Sheriff Peale pounced. "Is that true, Miss Brown? You've never been on Big Bear?" He whipped an object from his pocket. "This couldn't be yours, then?"

Penny looked at the piece of charcoal pencil and swallowed hard. "I guess it could be mine. I've been on Big Bear. You get a good view of Apple Valley from the top."

"Penny paints and draws," Martha explained, after giving Penny a stern look.

"Now we're getting somewhere," Sheriff Peale said. "This piece of charcoal was found near the sinkhole where Melissa's body was."

"What's that got to do with anything?" demanded Jake. "You can't think Penny had anything to do with this."

"It means *somebody* finally admits to being on the mountain, Mr. MacAfee. Perhaps your niece saw something that will aid our investigation. You'd like to help us catch this bad person, wouldn't you, Penny?"

Penny nodded, while gritting her teeth at his talk-down-to tone.

"Good! Now, Deputy Coombs says you roam these

mountains freely. Says you probably see and hear more than anybody around. So, tell me what you saw up there. Can you do that, Penny?''

''I saw apple trees in full bloom.''

''What else?''

''Nothing.''

''Nothing out of the ordinary? No one else up there?''

Penny gave her aunt and uncle an apologetic look. ''I only went up there one time. How would I know what's ordinary?'' The only thing she remembered seeing, besides the blossom clouds, was some odd grooves cut into a rock. She didn't think the sheriff would be interested in rock marks.

Relentlessly, Sheriff Peale kept asking questions.

Finally, Jake MacAfee lost his patience. ''Sheriff, I've raised my sister's girl since she was three. Never known Penny to lie. She says she don't know anything, she don't. So I'll thank you to stop bullying her.''

''I'll conduct this investigation in my own way, Mr. MacAfee,'' the sheriff snapped. ''Murder is a serious matter.''

''How do you know it was murder?'' Jake shot back. ''Maybe Melissa just wandered up there and had an accident.''

''It was no accident. The girl didn't bury herself.''

''I reckon not,'' Martha said, shuddering. ''Poor child.''

''You don't know the worst of it, I assure you, Mrs. MacAfee,'' the sheriff replied grimly. ''Now, Penny, did you see any of that bunch from the Shady Valley commune in the area?''

''No, sir,'' Penny answered with surprise. ''They stay pretty much to themselves. No bother to anyone.''

''I wouldn't be too sure of that, miss. These weirdos aren't always so peaceful. You'd do well to avoid them.

In fact, Mr. MacAfee, I think you should stop Penny from wandering around these mountains so freely."

"Might as well forbid the wind to blow," Jake said with a tight smile. "But I thank you for your concern."

Red crept from the sheriff's neck to his face. "I'm trying to do my job, Mr. MacAfee. With very little help from you good citizens, I might add."

"I can't tell you what I don't know," Penny said helplessly. "I'm real sorry about Melissa."

"We all are," Martha said.

Sheriff Peale clapped his wide-brimmed hat on his head. "I told my deputy this would be a waste of time. Good day!"

No one said anything until they heard his car roar away.

"Never should have elected that boy sheriff. He's been away from his roots too long," Jake grumbled. "He won't get answers by bullying people. Not around here."

"Do you know anything that might help?" Martha asked.

"No, Aunt Martha. And I don't think it's fair to pick on the Shady Valley folks either."

"Never caused us any bother," agreed Jake.

Every year after the apple harvest some members of the commune would come by and ask to glean the orchard. Jake was happy to oblige. He always said, "Good fruit shouldn't be wasted."

"I hate to think of a killer running loose," Martha said. "That's what you read about happening in big cities. Not up here."

"Now, Martha," chided Jake. "We have our share of murders. This isn't the Garden of Eden, you know."

"I know. Sad to say, we have some serpents," Martha replied and stood up. "Well, let's get supper on the table, Penny."

Penny picked up her backpack. "I'll wash up and be right down."

"Give yourself a lick and a promise," advised Jake. "I'm about to die of starvation."

Glancing at the clock, Penny smiled. Uncle Jake thought he'd dry up and blow away if he didn't eat promptly at five. "Looks like I have five whole minutes before disaster strikes," she said.

"Don't get smart, get moving," Jake ordered with a grin.

The faint aroma of paint and turpentine greeted Penny as she opened her door. The large, multiwindowed room had been added to the one-hundred-year-old farmhouse for her grandfather when arthritis had crippled him. It overlooked the east orchard and made Pawpaw feel like he was still part of things. After he died, she had claimed the room. Uncle Jake put in extra lights and shelves, even made her the sturdy easel where her latest effort was drying. This was home . . . her own private place. She sighed with contentment and went to wash up.

No one mentioned Sheriff Peale or Melissa Burke during the meal. Conversation was about the crop, when the migrant workers were expected, and other farm matters. Penny told of rescuing the greenhorn, but was otherwise silent. Melissa's face kept popping into her mind. That and the dreaded job at the Waysider.

"You're awful quiet tonight," Jake said, pushing away from the table. "You worried about that sheriff?"

"Not really. I don't know anything. Leastwise, I don't think I do. Guess I was thinking about tomorrow."

Jake caught the look that passed between Penny and Martha. "What happens tomorrow?"

"Elvira Hawkins needs help at the Waysider. The college kids will be going back soon," Martha said quickly. "She asked me at Circle last week if Penny could fill in."

"I can earn enough money for my art supplies," Penny added.

"I don't recollect asking you to do that," Jake said in a hurt voice. "Haven't we always bought what you need?"

"Sure, you have."

"It was my idea, Jake," Martha said. "Penny needs to be amongst other people more. She's too much of a solitary."

Jake smiled and shook his head. "I see you two already got this worked out."

"It's just a few hours on weekends," Penny said. "Just till tourist season's over, Uncle Jake."

"You take Rusty with you tomorrow," Martha said, frowning. "I don't want you out anywheres alone."

Penny laughed. "You think Miz Hawkins will like Rusty hanging around?"

"I don't care what Elvira likes. You take Rusty or you don't go tramping through these mountains," Martha said flatly. "Nobody'll bother you with him around."

"Okay." Then Penny said, "After I feed Rusty I'll take Uncle Arly's supper over to him."

"Add extra gravy," Martha reminded her. "Uncle Arly likes that."

Arly Carrier wasn't really kin. The eighty-nine-year-old lived alone a few hundred yards down the road. Independent and gnarly as last year's apples, was the way Jake described Uncle Arly. Only when Uncle Arly was almost blind would he agree to let Penny bring him "a bite of supper" each night. In exchange, he insisted the MacAfees cut firewood from his land free of charge.

Crusty or not, Penny liked the old man; taking him supper wasn't a chore but a pleasure. Sometimes he sat on his front porch to eat and told her stories about the early days in the mountains. Sometimes he told her about her mother—little Jenny—and all the mischief she and Jake had gotten into. Sometimes, when he was feeling poorly, he took the food, thanked her, and slipped back inside.

This evening was a "poorly" one. "Just set it by the door," Arly called out when she knocked. "Thank ya kindly."

"You're welcome. See you tomorrow." Penny knew better than to ask what was wrong or if he needed help. Uncle Arly was right tetchy about that.

When she returned to the house, the evening news was on and Uncle Jake was sound asleep in his recliner. Martha had her sewing basket out and was listening to but not watching the TV. "I'm going to do a little painting and turn in," Penny whispered.

"Get a good rest."

"You, too." Penny started down the hall, then turned back. "He isn't upset with me, is he?"

Martha shook her head. "You know he thinks the sun rises and sets on you. He'd keep things just the way they are, if he had his druthers."

"I'd like to keep things the way they are, too."

Martha looked up from her mending. "Honey, things don't ever stay the same. You're growin' up whether you like it or not. Time you spread your wings a little. A few hours away from here won't hurt you. You might even get something out of it."

"Uh-huh. Dishpan hands."

A snore—sounding suspiciously like a laugh—erupted from the recliner.

"Good night, Penny," Martha said firmly.

Suppressing a giggle, Penny went down the hall. Martha

and Jake were quite a pair. She couldn't have picked better stand-in parents. She loved them dearly. Childless, they'd raised her like their own.

Martha was probably right about the job, Penny thought, as she unpacked her backpack and took out her new sketches. Somebody with a proper job wouldn't need to finish school, would they? This job could be her ticket out of boredom.

The sketch of the narrow little valley caught her eye. Putting up a fresh canvas, Penny began to paint.

Two hours later she threw her brush down in frustration. Something was wrong. No matter how hard she tried, the picture in the sketch and in her head would not go down on canvas! Shadows crept in where none existed.

Penny rubbed the back of her neck. Maybe she was just tired. She'd let it go for a while. Go to bed. Tomorrow was another day. What happened then could change her whole life. That is, if the plan forming in her head worked.

CHAPTER THREE

Penny smoothed her hair and retucked her blouse. Running her tongue over dry lips, she said, "Stay, Rusty. I don't think I'll be long." Taking a deep breath, she walked out of the woods and across the crowded parking lot of the Waysider.

Located just off the Blue Ridge Parkway, the Waysider was a popular eating place for tourists and locals. The sprawling, rustic restaurant was usually packed from early April through October.

The aroma of frying country ham and a babble of voices greeted Penny as she opened the door.

"Hi, Penny," someone called.

Looking across the room, Penny felt as if she'd been kicked in the stomach. "Hi, Ina Mae. Is Miz Hawkins around?"

"In the gift shop. Want me to show you?"

"I know where it is," Penny replied, turning too quickly and bumping into a departing customer. "Excuse me."

Ina Mae Akers always had the same effect on her! Every time she saw Ina Mae she remembered that awful day on the playground . . . girls jumping rope . . . Ina Mae and

Sue Ellen turning and chanting, "Penelope Brown is a clown. Sees her letters upside down." Everyone else was laughing. Ina Mae made it clear what everyone was thinking. Penny didn't belong with the third graders anymore. Dumb, slow Penny hadn't been promoted with the rest of her class. She'd had to stay in second grade until she learned to read and write properly. It was the first time she'd known she was stupid. The hurt still hadn't gone away.

"Penny, were you looking for me?"

The voice jerked her back to the present. "Uh—yes, Miz Hawkins."

"Well, come on in here where we can talk. We're not too busy yet. Breakfast folks don't buy many souvenirs. How're Martha and Jake?"

"Just fine." Penny followed Miz Hawkins's ample body into a small shop filled with mountain crafts.

"Looks like we'll have a bumper crop of apples and tourists this year, don't it? Our trees are full to breaking. And the weather's been just right for fall coloring, don't you think?"

"Yes, ma'am," Penny answered, holding in a sigh. She may not be able to read words easily, but she sure could read faces. Miz Hawkins was flushed and babbling like a brook. "I came about the job, Miz Hawkins."

Her round face looking like an overripe tomato, Miz Hawkins said, "I know, honey. And I just hate to tell you, but Ham hired Ina Mae yesterday. He wanted somebody who could help out front in a pinch, not just in the kitchen. You know, run the cash register, take orders, and such. Ina Mae's—uh—in high school. He figured she'd do better. I'm real sorry."

"That's okay, Miz Hawkins," Penny said, swallowing her hurt.

The woman chattered on. "I told Ham he was making a mistake. You wouldn't be asking time off for football games and dates. A pretty girl like Ina Mae's bound to be popular."

"Thanks for thinking of me," Penny said, turning to go.

A flustered Miz Hawkins followed on her heels. "Not that you aren't pretty, honey. I didn't mean that. It's just that—uh—well, like Ina Mae said, she's better qualified for the job."

"I understand." She caught a display of baskets before they tumbled to the floor. "It's okay. Really."

"You come see me next spring and we'll find some job better suited to you. Okay?"

"Sure." Penny smiled brightly at the woman and tried to get out of the shop without knocking over anything else.

"Bye-bye, Penny," Ina Mae sang out.

Penny pretended she didn't hear. She kept her back straight and her face blank until she reached the woods. Then she kicked a pine cone so hard it ricocheted off three trees. So much for her grand plan! Why did people think if you couldn't read you were dumb? If they said it often enough you could even believe it yourself!

Rusty whined and licked her hand.

"Sorry, boy. I'm not mad at you," she said, stroking his head. "Come on, let's get back where we belong."

She was still fuming over the injustice when she reached Fox Hollow and saw Chris Williams lounging against the fence under the Fox Hollow Orchard sign. "What are you doing here?"

A grin played hide-and-seek on his face. "Waiting for you."

"How'd you find me?"

Chris waved a folded paper in front of her. "You said Fox Hollow. I went over to the Fire and Rescue Station.

Figured they'd have maps. The rest was simple, I asked people. Your mom wasn't sure when you'd be back, but I thought I'd take a chance and wait."

He looked so pleased with himself, she had to smile. "That was my Aunt Martha, not my mom. Why go to all the trouble?"

"You disappeared yesterday before I could thank you."

Penny shrugged. "No thanks needed."

"Wrong! You saved my butt. I have to admit I was ticked at you running off ... until I figured out why. You're pretty sharp, Penelope."

"Oh, sure."

"Hey, if you'd led me into Glyn Ayr everyone would've known I'd been lost. I didn't think of that, but you did."

"But—"

Chris held up a large hand. "No buts. Except mine. Which you saved. And I thank you."

His smile was infectious. You couldn't stay cross with a smile like that. "You're welcome."

"You wouldn't want to do it again, would you? Save me, I mean."

"Are you planning on getting lost again?"

"Not if you'll teach me how to navigate in these mountains."

"Me?"

For a split second, yesterday's panic flashed in his eyes. "Yeah. These mountains give me the creeps. They're so ... so wild. No people. No signs to guide you. Just trees, rocks, and briars."

"Just stay in town like most of the other kids do," she advised, walking away.

"I'd like to, but I can't," Chris said, matching her stride for stride.

"Why not?"

"I have a good reason, believe me."

Something in his voice made Penny stop. She turned and searched his face. This was really important to him. "Okay. It isn't all that hard. When do you want to start?"

"The sooner, the better. Can you work me in around your new job?"

"I didn't get the job," Penny snapped.

"Bummer! Someone beat you to it?"

Penny remembered Ina Mae's smirky smile. "You could say that. It's okay. I didn't want to be cooped up every weekend anyway. How about tomorrow?"

"Super! What time? My place or yours?"

"I'll be by your house about nine," she said quickly. No use asking for a teasing. "Wear long pants and some sturdy shoes this time."

Chris looked down at his sandaled feet and grinned. "Gotcha, Teach. See ya at nine." With a final pat on Rusty's head, he ambled away.

Now what have I gotten myself into? Penny wondered, watching him go off with a coltish gait. Why should I care whether he likes my mountains or not? But somehow, she did care. Besides, teaching him to be at home in her world might be fun. "At least it's something I'm qualified to do," she said aloud.

Explaining the job—or lack of one—to Martha wasn't going to be easy. Anyone who treated Penny badly had better be ready to answer to Martha. Even her church friends. Martha was as protective as a mama cat with new kittens. Penny had learned to keep her hurts and slights to herself. So she pasted a smile on her face when she went into the house. "Yoo-hoo! I'm back."

"In here," Martha called from the kitchen. "When do you start work? Did your young man find you?"

"Would you believe Mr. Hawkins had already hired

someone?'' Penny said breezily. "Miz Hawkins apologized for him going behind her back. And, yes, Chris found me. But he's not *my* young man."

"Ham already hired somebody? Who?"

"Ina Mae Akers. She was already working. Good luck to her, I say. Place was too crowded and noisy for me. Couldn't hear myself think."

"Um-m," Martha said, eyeing Penny carefully. "What did the boy want? He seemed real anxious."

"He's the fellow I rescued yesterday. Lives in the old Wilcox place. Seems like he's afraid of these wild mountains. Wants me to teach him how to get around in them so he won't get lost again. I said I would."

Martha looked flabbergasted. "You did?"

"Sure. Why not? Who knows this place better?"

"Nobody," Martha replied. "Did you say the Wilcox place? I thought that fellow who had the accident bought the Wilcox's."

"He did. That was Chris's uncle. He died and left the place to his sister—Chris's mom."

True to mountain custom, Martha began quizzing Penny about Chris's family. "Where'd they come from? What's his daddy do? How come they moved up here?"

"Whoa, Aunt Martha," Penny said, laughing. "Near as I can tell it's just Chris and his mom that are here. When I rescued Chris I didn't think to ask his family history."

"Family is important," Martha replied.

"I know that. But it's not like I plan to marry Chris. I'm only going to show him how to get around in these hills."

"Well," Martha conceded, "I reckon there's no harm in that."

"No harm at all. After tomorrow I'm sure I won't see much of Chris Williams."

"Why not?"

"He's in high school," Penny answered testily. "Why would he hang around an eighth grader?"

Martha opened her mouth to say something, but Penny cut her off. "You want me to pick tomatoes today?"

"I picked yesterday. But you could get us some corn."

"Done," Penny said and let herself out the back door. Suddenly she didn't want to think about high school students, cute or not.

Unfortunately, the three regular orchard workers wouldn't let her forget. Chris had asked them for directions. During the noon meal, the three teased Penny unmercifully about the "good-looking city boy who was hankerin' after her."

The more Penny tried to explain, the more they teased. Finally, Martha said, "Enough!"

Penny gave her a grateful look and escaped to her room. Today that stubborn glen would come out right!

It did not. The shadows remained.

CHAPTER FOUR

River Road was the prettiest section of Glyn Ayr, in Penny's opinion. Large sycamores, oaks, and maples arched over the narrow lane, providing a tunnel of cool shade. Little River gurgled along on the right, and on the left were four of the town's oldest homes. The Wilcox place—Chris's house—was the last one. The driveway up to the two-story, rose brick house was lined with old boxwoods.

Rusty had to investigate each and every pungent shrub.

Chris was waiting on the wide front steps. Today he was properly dressed. "Hi," he said, turning around for her inspection. "How's this?"

"Much better," Penny said, feeling awkward after yesterday's teasing. "You ready?"

Chris grinned and slung a lumpy book bag over his shoulder. "Lead on, Teach."

In spite of his jolly tone, Penny could see he was nervous. "You want to hike some trails around here?"

"Yeah. Easy ones, if that's possible."

"Okay. We'll take Mossy Creek." She led him back down the drive and plunged into the forest, weaving confidently through the trees. "It'll be easier when we join the parkway's cleared trail. Mossy Creek trail is marked with yellow blazes."

Chris followed as close as Rusty's wagging tail would allow. "You never told me your dog's name," he said. "I'll bet it's Shadow."

"You lose. It's Rusty."

"Hah! It should be Shadow. Wherever you go he's right beside you."

"Except at school. He's banned from school property."

"Why?"

Penny patted Rusty. "He used to come every day, didn't you, boy? He'd wait all day in the school yard, then beat my bus home. Until one day at recess, this boy chased me in a game of tag. We fell and Rusty thought I was being hurt. In a flash he was all over Freddy, shaking him like he was a rag doll. Freddy wet his pants."

Chris chuckled. "Bet Freddy left you alone after that."

"No, he didn't. It turned into a game and got rougher. When three boys cornered me, Rusty took a bite outta one. That's when he got banned."

"Bummer! He was just protecting you."

"That's what I tried to tell the principal. Didn't work. He said Rusty was dangerous."

"People can be stupid."

"Stupid or not, Rusty stays home," Penny muttered as they reached a wide trail.

After a few minutes, they came to a fork in the path. Chris followed her without comment. Penny frowned. Gradually, she veered off the track and after a few yards halted. "Okay, Chris, think you can find your way back home?"

Panic darkened his blue eyes. "There's no trail! How'd we get here?"

"I stepped off a little while ago. You were following

me. You were *not* watching where you were going,'' Penny scolded.

"We were talking."

"You have to pay attention out here, Chris. I told you Mossy Creek was blazed in yellow. Did you even notice when the trail forked which branch we took?"

Chris shook his head. Beads of sweat glistened on his brow. "Yellow blaze, less talking, more looking. Got it."

Penny sighed. "Chris, why are you doing this? You can live in Glyn Ayr without ever going into the mountains."

"Sure I could," Chris said, looking stubborn. "But I don't want to. Okay?"

"Okay."

From then on, he paid close attention as she pointed out odd groups of trees, rock formations, and plants to use for landmarks. "Turn and look over your shoulder every once in a while," she advised.

"Why? Are we being followed?"

"No. You want to know how it looks coming back. It won't be the same."

"How'd you learn all this?" Chris asked, panting slightly as the trail wound upward.

"Practice. I've been doing this since I was four or five."

"You never got lost?"

Penny giggled and slowed her pace. "Once. When I was six I wandered clear over to Jordan Mountain. Turkey Collins found me and took me home before anyone missed me. He never told on me either."

Her answer seemed to make Chris feel better. "You always do this alone?"

Penny nodded. "Aunt Martha says I'm a solitary."

"A what?"

"Solitary. Means I like my own company best." As she spoke, the trail broke out of the trees into a high meadow filled with black-eyed Susans and bisected by a meandering stream.

Chris let out a low whistle of admiration.

"This isn't even the best part," Penny assured him. "Wait till we get to Raven Overlook."

"Hold on!" Chris said, flopping down in the shade and unslinging his book bag. "Let's take five. I brought us a snack."

"It's nowhere near lunchtime," Penny protested.

"Lunch—smunch. I'm always hungry. Mom says I have hollow legs."

"You can't possibly have enough in that little ole bag to fill those legs," Penny said, sitting beside him.

"Maybe its magic. Like this meadow," Chris said.

The bag wasn't magic, but it yielded more than Penny imagined. Chris wolfed down his share quickly. "You were right," he said, standing and shaking one of his legs. "It's only half full."

"You should have a bigger bag or a smaller appetite," Penny said, laughing.

"I'm sure Uncle Pat had some gear stashed around. I just haven't found it yet. Here you go, Rusty," he said, holding out the crusts of his sandwich.

Rusty turned away.

"He won't take food from anyone but me," Penny said.

"Why not?"

"A few years back some crazy was going around the county throwing out poisoned meat. Uncle Jake helped me train Rusty so he'd be safe." She took the bread from Chris. "Here, boy."

"Okay, Teach, which way now?" Chris asked.

"You tell me."

Chris scanned the meadow until he saw a yellow blaze on a tree across the way. "We go that-a-way, ma'am."

"See? It's not so hard," Penny said, smiling.

"Yeah. Right. *If* you happen to be on a marked trail."

"You said start easy," she reminded him. "Wilderness hiking takes a little more time and skill."

"Guess that's what I was doing the other day. There weren't any trails—marked or otherwise—when I got lost."

"Yes, there were. You just weren't looking. That's what happens to nine out of ten people who get lost."

Chris gave her a lopsided grin. "Guess I should be happy to be with the majority, huh?"

After a long, steep climb they reached Raven Overlook where a vast emerald quilt of trees spread out as far as the eye could see. Instead of being impressed, Chris seemed daunted by the view. "Sure is a lot of trees. Is all of this in Wayne County?"

"Most of it. Why?"

"No reason," he answered. "Let's go back."

"You lead this time," Penny said. To make conversation, she asked, "Was your uncle a big outdoorsman? Hiking, fishing, hunting, I mean?"

"Not really. His move up here surprised Mom and me. When we found out where he'd disappeared to, that is."

"Disappeared? Wasn't your mom close to her brother?"

"Close? Mom and Uncle Pat were twins. You can't get much closer than that! Uncle Pat was more like a father to me than my own dad. We three spent a lot of time together . . . until Grampa Moore died." Pain thickened Chris's voice.

"What happened?"

Chris shrugged helplessly. "We don't know. Uncle Pat resigned from the university and just disappeared! Oh, we got postcards from time to time. From first one place, then another. Then, out of the blue, we got a brief note saying he'd bought a house in Glyn Ayr and was remodeling it. We didn't hear another word until the hospital called us."

"Gee, that is strange," was all she could think to say.

"According to my great-aunt Emma, the family genealogist, there's been one 'strange' male in every generation of Moores. She said Uncle Pat was following the family tradition."

Penny heard the disbelief in his voice. "But you don't think so?"

"I don't know what I think. Not yet."

A group of hikers came along just then and when they had passed, Chris changed the subject. "So tell me about life in the Blue Ridge. What do you guys do for fun?"

Although she didn't consider herself one of the guys, Penny knew what went on. She told him and asked about life in Alexandria.

Chris gave a rather funny account of big-city life. Then somehow he got on to his favorite hobby: computers. He was so busy telling her the wonders of these machines that he missed the cutoff to River Road. Penny kept quiet. Better to let him learn from his mistake.

When they reached the paved road, Chris gave her a sheepish grin. "I blew it, huh?"

"You just missed the last turn. Know where we are?"

"Route Five. Just above River Road. We musta passed right behind my house," he said, disgustedly. "I'm hopeless."

"It's okay, Chris. You weren't paying attention when we started."

"Or when we finished. For sure, I'm no Daniel Bo—"

His words were cut off by the wail of a siren. A brown cruiser pulled in front of them. Sheriff Peale got out and slammed the door. "Come here. I want to talk to you."

Penny and Chris stepped forward.

"Not you. Her."

Penny—with Rusty beside her—obeyed.

Sheriff Peale gave her a tight-lipped smile. "Maybe we can talk better without your folks around."

"I already told you everything I know."

"You didn't mention the fight you had with Melissa."

Penny paled. "Where did you hear about that?"

The sheriff smiled wolfishly. "I talked with some of your classmates. Seems like you and Melissa didn't get along. Want to tell me about this fight?"

"It wasn't a fight. Melissa didn't want me on the Halloween decorating committee. She called me a retard!"

"And you told her she'd be sorry!"

Penny looked him in the eye. "I meant about the decorating. That committee could have used my help. I'm good at art."

"You weren't even a little angry at being called a retard?"

She couldn't control the telltale flush on her face, but she answered calmly. "I'm used to it. Melissa wasn't the first . . . or the last."

"Don't lie to me! Everyone said you were furious. You wanted to get back at Melissa, didn't you? Did you lure her into the woods as a joke? Or at someone else's suggestion?"

Penny was too stunned to reply. But Rusty bared his teeth and growled at Sheriff Peale's tone.

"Hold that dog or I'll shoot him!" the sheriff yelled.

"You wouldn't do that in front of a witness, would you?" Chris asked, coming to stand beside Penny.

"Back off, city boy! This doesn't concern you."

"Proper police procedure should concern every citizen," Chris retorted. "Your procedure is questionable."

For a minute Penny thought the sheriff would strike

Chris. Instead, he put his clenched fists on his hips and glared at her. "If you had anything—anything at all—to do with this murder, I'll find out. And retarded or not, you *will* be prosecuted." With a crisp about-face, he stalked back to the patrol car and drove off.

Penny managed a weak smile. "You sounded like a lawyer, Chris."

"Probably because I've been around a few. My father's a lawyer. Guess he's a good one. He sure screwed Mom in the divorce. Come on, let's get outta here."

They moved back into the shelter of the trees.

"Why's Attila the Hun on your case, Penny?"

She told him about Melissa.

"That's it? A piece of charcoal and a few angry words? He's blowing smoke! I knew that guy was a jerk the first time I met him."

"Where'd you meet Sheriff Peale?"

"In his office. I dropped by to see the report on Uncle Pat's accident."

"And?"

"There wasn't one. Man fell, was rescued, sent to Roanoke Hospital, died two months later. Why bother with a lot of paperwork?"

Penny frowned. "What did you hope to find?"

A guarded look slid over Chris's face. "I just wanted to see the report. Guess I got a little steamed at the sheriff."

"I don't think Sheriff Peale has a very high opinion of kids," Penny said wryly.

"You can say that again. What's with this retarded bit? What right does he have to say that?"

Penny sighed. Everyone found out sooner or later so she might as well get it out in the open. "I'm fifteen and in the eighth grade. I was held back because I have something called dyslexia. It makes me have trouble reading."

46

"Jeez, Louise!" Chris said. "Dyslexia isn't retardation. I had a classmate at Belmont who was dyslexic. No big deal."

"It *is* a big deal around here. Most folks don't know what dyslexia is. They think you're either lazy or retarded!"

"That's their problem. Not yours."

"It's *my* problem," Penny lashed out, "when they stick me in a 'special' class so I won't hold back the normal kids! You know how that makes you feel? Like the bad apple in a barrel. Even when they put you back in class with everyone else, the dummy label sticks like glue!"

Chris stepped back from her anger. "I never thought of it that way."

"Well, that's the way it is."

"But it shouldn't be," Chris protested. "You are not retarded and you ought not to let people get away with that kind of talk."

Penny stopped dead in her tracks. Who did he think he was, telling her how to behave? "How I act is none of your business, Chris Williams! Now, if you want to get home go down this path about fifty yards and hang a right. You'll be in your own backyard." She wheeled sharply and promptly fell over Rusty.

Chris burst out laughing.

Echoes of cruel playground laughter filled her head. Penny picked herself up, thrusting away Chris's hand. "Leave me alone."

"I'm sorry. You did a super prat fall...."

"Thanks." She started off with as much dignity as she could muster.

"How about another lesson? Maybe Labor Day? If you're not busy, that is."

"We go to Roanoke shopping on Labor Day."

"Okay. I'll see you Tuesday at school," Chris called hopefully.

"No, you won't," Penny replied over her shoulder. "You go to the high school between here and Bramer. I'm still at Jefferson." She crossed the road and disappeared into the woods.

She was almost home before she simmered down and realized how silly she'd been. What on earth was wrong with her? Chris didn't understand how things worked up here. Changing mountain opinions was about as easy as roping the wind. How was he supposed to know that?

"Well, that's the end of that friendship," she told Rusty. "Would've ended soon anyway. School starts Tuesday. Chris will find a whole bunch of friends in high school. Right?"

Rusty had stopped with his nose in the air, sniffing. A low growl rumbled in his throat as a flash of sunlight came from the adjoining woods.

"Don't be silly, boy," Penny scolded. "It's only the sun on some birdwatcher's binoculars. Doesn't concern us. Let's enjoy our last day of freedom."

Reluctantly, Rusty followed her.

From a safe distance, so did someone else.

CHAPTER FIVE

The truck's headlights cut through the inky darkness. Long gone were the bright city lights. Penny squenched between Jake and Martha, exhausted. Except for buying her art supplies, she found the shopping trip boring. The hastily eaten french fries and Big Mac sat uneasily on the stomach.

At last, Jake pulled up by their front steps. "Y'all unload the house stuff. I'll take the tractor parts 'round back."

Gratefully, Martha and Penny climbed down and stretched. Usually they took the car, but this time Jake needed to buy some farm supplies.

"Hurry along," Jake growled.

"You just hold your horses, Jake MacAfee," Martha snapped. "I gotta get the kinks out."

"I wonder where Rusty is?" Penny said, looking around the yard. "He's usually here to meet us."

Martha grabbed some packages. "Lordy, I hope he's not chasing the Parkers' chickens. I couldn't put up with Vera's squawking tonight."

Penny chuckled. Vera Parker did sound like her banty

hens when she was riled. She unloaded the rest of the packages. Still no Rusty. Feeling uneasy, she put two fingers in her mouth and whistled. There was no responding bark or flash of black fur.

"Don't fret. He's around someplace. Come on, let's get this stuff put away."

Reluctantly, Penny followed her aunt inside. Something didn't feel right.

They'd just finished sorting things when Jake stormed in. "Dad-blamed, no good bastard's struck again! Both barn cats are dead. I found this beside Hector." He held up a stick with a chunk of raw meat on it.

"Rusty!" Penny yelled and dived for the door.

Jake was right behind her.

They found Rusty beside the upper fence. He was barely breathing. White foam covered his dark muzzle.

Jake scooped up the dog and staggered toward the house. "Tell Martha to call Doc Carter. Get that piece of meat and meet me by the truck."

Penny ran like a deer.

The trip to the animal clinic was the longest ride Penny had ever taken. She cradled Rusty's head in her lap, bathing his face with her tears.

The wiry veterinarian was waiting for them. He held the door open and directed Jake into the surgery. With gentle, skilled fingers he probed and examined Rusty's inert form. "Maced ... or something like it," he said grimly. "He's not been poisoned though."

Penny forced words between her dry lips. "Is he gonna die?"

"Not if I can help it," Doc said. He put an odd-shaped mask over Rusty's muzzle. "The chemical slowed down his respiratory system. Oxygen will help him breathe. Talk to him, Penny. I need to wash this gunk out of his eyes."

Accompanied by the soft hiss of oxygen, Penny began talking. Finally, Rusty's tail gave a feeble thump. It was the most beautiful thing she had ever seen.

"Keep talking," Doc ordered, as he repeatedly sluiced the dog's eyes.

"Is he blind?" Jake asked softly.

"Temporarily. That's why I want Penny to keep reassuring him."

Finally, Doc Carter removed the mask and Rusty breathed on his own. His cloudy eyes looked blank, but his pink tongue gave the vet's hand a quick lick. "I think that's got it. Open that crate, Jake. Let's move him over."

"Can I stay with him?" Penny pled.

"No need. He'll sleep now. I'm right next door and I'll check on him. He's strong and healthy. The blindness is temporary, I'm sure. You can pick him up tomorrow."

"He'll do better if I stay with him," Penny said stubbornly.

Jake took her arm. "Listen to Doc, honey. Rusty's in good hands. He'll be okay."

"Only because you got him here when you did," Doc said. "What kind of sick S.O.B. would do this? Did you bring that meat, Jake?"

"It's in the truck. I'll get it," Jake said.

Penny stayed by the crate, stroking Rusty's paw through the wires.

"I'll send this to the lab in the morning," Doc said when Jake returned. "Wash your hands good, Jake. You, too, Penny. You best call the sheriff, Jake."

"Soon as I get home. Come on, Penny."

"Thanks, Doc," Penny said, with one last look at Rusty.

"No thanks needed."

Martha had more bad news when Jake and Penny returned. "Someone tried to break in," she said angrily. "I found the screen pried off Penny's window."

Jake marched to the phone and called the sheriff's office. "He's coming right over."

Utterly drained, Penny knew she couldn't face Sheriff Peale and be civil. "I'm going up to bed."

Penny's body went to school Tuesday morning. Her mind didn't. She moved through the day like a robot, following her classmates from one room to another. All she could think about was Rusty.

When the last bell finally rang she made a beeline for the entrance. She was halfway down the walk when she saw the familiar brown car parked behind the line of yellow buses. Sheriff Peale lounged against the front fender. She knew he was waiting for her. Not today! No way! She threw her shoulders back and raced on.

"Whoa, missy!" Sheriff Peale stepped in front of her. "I want to talk to you."

She tried to sidestep, but he blocked her easily. "I have to go get my dog!"

"That's what I'm here about. This time it was your dog. Next time it could be you ... if someone thinks you know something."

"That's ridiculous!"

"Then why break into your room?"

"Because it's at the back of the house," Penny snapped. "Any fool knows that. Let me pass."

Sheriff Peale grabbed her shoulder. "You sure you don't have something tucked away?"

Twisting from his grasp, Penny yelled, "I don't *know* anything!" She dodged around him and ran. She felt hundreds of curious eyes stabbing her back.

Rounding a corner on the town square, she ran smack

into the high school students getting off the bus. They jostled her and closed ranks.

"Hey, watch it!"

"What's your hurry?"

"Where's the fire?"

Almost in tears, Penny fought back. Suddenly her path was cleared. Someone was running beside her. Penny glanced over and saw Chris, matching her stride for stride. He didn't say a word, simply kept pace.

"Thanks," she said when they reached the animal clinic.

"None needed." He opened the door for her. "Rusty?"

Penny nodded. "Hi, Mrs. Carter. Is—"

A glad bark answered her. A second later, Rusty raced from the back into her arms.

Doc Carter followed at a more leisurely pace. "As you can see, he's fine, Penny."

Penny raised her head from Rusty's fur. "Thanks, Doc."

"My pleasure."

"Is he really okay?"

"Well, he may be hungry. He drank some water, but I couldn't get him to eat."

Penny smiled. "Good, boy. That's what saved his life, Doc. He won't take food from anyone but me."

"I wondered about that. Not many dogs would pass up a piece of sirloin. I sent it off to the lab, by the way."

"Anyone else lose any animals?" Penny asked.

"Not that I've heard about. Been expecting calls all day. So far, you are the only ones hit."

"Good. Uncle Jake'll be by in a few minutes to settle up. Is it okay if we go outside to wait?"

"You run along. I'll bill Jake later."

As soon as they were seated on a grassy bank, Chris said, "Fill me in."

Briefly, Penny told him what had happened.

"Jeez, I thought we left crime behind. Although, someone did break into Uncle Pat's while he was in the hospital. Nothing was taken though," Chris said. "Hey, you don't think the sheriff could be right do you?"

"About what?"

"About someone thinking you know something."

Penny shook her head. "There's no connection. Lots of people know we go to Roanoke on Labor Day. Perfect time for a burglary. But first you'd have to get rid of Rusty."

"Yeah, I guess."

"If I can figure it out, it looks like that dumb sheriff could! I wish he'd stop harping on Melissa."

"Maybe something about her death has him worried. Wonder what?"

Penny shrugged. "It's a mystery to me."

"I hate mysteries!" Chris said vehemently. "I can't rest until they're solved."

"You mean about your uncle?" Penny asked, watching his troubled face.

"Yeah. Mom thinks I'm nuts. But she didn't hear all Uncle Pat said." Abruptly, Chris stood up. "I called you Sunday and Monday but never got an answer."

"Sorry. We had a church picnic on Sunday, then the shopping trip."

"You think I could talk you into another lesson, Penny?"

She took one look at his serious face and said, "Sure. When?"

"How about Saturday?"

"Okay," she said as a horn tootled. "My ride's here."

54

"Hi, honey," Martha called as they approached the car. "Sorry you had to wait. The pickers came a day early and Jake had his hands full. I came as soon as I could. Rusty okay?"

"Doc says he's fine." Penny put Rusty into the backseat. "Chris, I think we'd better hold up on Saturday. With the picking starting, Aunt Martha'll need me around."

"Okay," he said, looking disappointed. "I'll give you a call."

"Okay. And thanks again for the company."

"Anytime."

"He seems like a nice boy," Martha said as they drove off.

"He is." But he sure has something bugging him, she added silently. "How many workers came in? Is Ernesto still the crew boss?"

"Seventeen. And Ernesto's back," Martha replied. "He asked about you first thing. Said his wife loved your painting. Now she can't forget him while he's away."

"Nobody could forget that happy face," Penny said. But she was pleased. Not many people outside her family ever saw any of her work. It was nice to know it was appreciated.

Uncle Arly did not have a happy face when Penny took him his supper that evening. He was waiting on the porch, thumping his cane impatiently. " 'Bout time you got here," he grumbled. "What's goin' on up to your place?"

Penny put his tray on the table. "Oh, the pickers came today. You know how that is."

"Didn't mean that! What happened yesterday?"

"Someone tried to break in while we were in Roanoke. They threw out some poisoned meat. Killed two of our cats. But Rusty prevented anyone from getting in, even if he did get a faceful of Mace.''

More wrinkles crowded Uncle Arly's face. ''I knowed it was sumpin' bad! I got a whiff of brimstone long about sundown.'' His rheumy eyes peered fearfully at Penny. ''You folks a'right?''

''We're fine, Uncle Arly. Did you see anyone hanging around?''

He shook his head. ''Eyesight's turrible. Nothing wrong with my nose, though. The devil was walkin' last night, Penny. I smelled 'im.''

Penny hid a smile. ''I'll tell Sheriff Peale to look for someone with body odor.''

''Don't you be funnin' at me, missy,'' Uncle Arly said, wagging a bony finger at her. ''Evil has a smell. Y'all best go wary.''

''We'll be careful,'' Penny assured him. ''Now eat your supper before it gets cold. One cold meal a week is enough.''

''Them ham biscuits was jist fine. I'm partial to 'em. Did I tell you 'bout the time my whole fambly had nuthin' to eat but acorns?''

Penny settled down in a rocker. ''No, sir.''

Between bites, Uncle Arly told her the story once again. Reliving the old days made him forget his devil-walking fears.

Satisfied, Penny forgot, too.

CHAPTER SIX

"Come sit with us, Penny," Peggy Sue invited.

"We saved you a place," Adele said, patting a chair at the lunch table.

Mary Beth smiled sympathetically. "We sure were sorry about your dog. I hope Sheriff Peale catches that low-down varmit."

Penny wasn't fooled by the sudden friendliness of the town trio. With an apologetic glance at her usual lunch group, she took the offered seat. "So do I. But I wouldn't count on it. Sheriff Peale seems to look in all the wrong places for answers."

Peggy Sue giggled nervously. "Yeah, he does, don't he?"

The other two girls nodded vigorously.

Penny began eating, waiting to see where they'd go next.

Mary Beth, the self-appointed leader of the pack, pulled a long face. "Would you believe he asked us about that little spat you had with poor Melissa? Imagine him thinking *that* was important!"

"I can't imagine," Penny said. "I did wonder who told him about it though."

All three girls reddened.

"He said any little thing," Adele blurted.

"We just wanted to help," Peggy Sue added.

Penny picked at the tasteless glob on her plate. "The sheriff's wasting his time looking in my direction. I don't know any more than you do."

"See?" Mary Beth said. "I told y'all Sheriff Peale was barkin' up the wrong tree." Peggy Sue and Adele opened their mouths to protest, but Mary Beth continued quickly. "My daddy says Sheriff Peale better get off his rear end and find out something or he won't be sheriff come next election. Two girls missing in this county and one of 'em dead is no kind of record to run on."

Penny put her fork down. "Two? Who was the other one?"

Mary Beth bristled with importance. Her father was on the county board of supervisors, which gave her special status. "Tanya Blevins. Over in Shady Valley. Everybody thinks she just ran off when her mama remarried, but no one's seen or heard from her in two years."

"All this scary stuff's ruining my appetite," Peggy Sue complained. "Let's talk about something else. What all did you do this summer, Penny?"

"Nothing much," Penny replied.

"We went to Myrtle Beach," Mary Beth said. "I met some real cute boys down there."

"Speaking of cute boys," Adele chimed in, "where did you meet Chris Williams, Penny?"

Aha! Penny thought. Now she knew what the girls wanted. It wasn't hard to figure out that the three of them had rehearsed this scene. "I met Chris out hiking in the mountains. I find lots of good things out there. You should try it sometime."

"O-o-o-o, if I thought I'd catch something that cute, I

surely would," Peggy Sue said, practically drooling in her milk.

"I hear he's a superbrain. Mama teaches at the high school, you know," Adele said, preening. "He got put in all the advanced classes."

"Oh, who cares if he's smart," Mary Beth said loftily. "What's he like, Penny?"

Not accustomed to this girl talk, Penny answered literally. "He likes computers." Then, without hesitation, she rattled off Chris's passionate explanation of computer technology.

All three girls rolled their eyes heavenward.

"I didn't know you were such a computer fan," Mary Beth said caustically.

Penny blushed. Recalling word for word what she heard was the way she learned. She realized she'd captured Chris's enthusiasm in her repetition. "I'm not. You asked what he liked. I told you."

Adele and Peggy Sue giggled.

"No, Penny," Mary Beth said with exaggerated patience, "we meant what kind of guy is Chris?"

"Nice."

"He's really tall. Does he play basketball?" Adele asked.

"I—I don't know. I don't think so," Penny replied.

Peggy Sue leaned across the table. "He wears dishy designer jeans. Is he rich?"

"When's his daddy coming? Or is he?" Mary Beth said with a smirk. "I heard his mama was divorced."

"What do y'all find to talk about?" asked Peggy Sue.

Head swimming from their curiosity, Penny picked up her tray. "I don't ask personal questions. Excuse me." She walked away, leaving the town trio gawking.

She was not as calm and collected as she seemed. She

knew everyone was wondering what a smart guy like Chris was doing hanging out with a dummy like her. Nothing went unnoticed in this small community. After yesterday's act of friendship, she and Chris were firmly linked in everyone's mind. Poor Chris. She hoped he wasn't being teased too hard. Guys could be just as cruel as girls when it came to teasing.

"Well, at least he has an out," she muttered to herself. "He doesn't have to call me. I don't think he will either."

Penny underestimated Chris. He phoned her that evening and continued to keep in touch. Twice during the next two busy weeks he ambled out to Fox Hollow. He made himself right at home with Martha and Jake, too. Oddest of all, he persuaded her to show him some of her artwork.

"She's good, Mrs. MacAfee," Chris said enthusiastically, after seeing Penny's paintings. "She ought to be showing in art galleries."

"Tell *her,* Chris," Martha said. "She don't show her work to hardly anybody."

"I'm not that good," Penny protested. "Sometimes I can't even paint what I see."

Chris helped himself to another handful of oatmeal cookies. "I'm no expert, but I think you're better than some of the stuff I've seen in the galleries."

"Better listen to him, Penny," Jake said. "He was smart enough to figure out the glitch in my computer."

"It isn't the same thing at all!" Penny said, red-faced.

"You're right," Chris agreed. "Computers I know. With art, I just know what I like. You don't have to share your talent with anyone. But I'd sure like for someone with more knowledge than me to see them."

"No!" She was torn between pleasure and anger—pleased that he enjoyed her work, angry at the spot he'd put her in. How could she explain in front of Martha and Jake that no one would show the work of a retard? People would only laugh at her pretending to be an artist. That would hurt Aunt Martha and Uncle Jake more than it would hurt her! "Y'all couldn't be just a little prejudiced, could you? It's just a hobby for me. Come on, Chris. I'll walk you to the road."

"Great cookies, Mrs. MacAfee," Chris said. "Wait up, Penny." He ran out the back door after her. "Jeez, don't be mad. I didn't mean to pressure you."

"It's okay. I'm glad you like my stuff."

"We're still on for tomorrow, aren't we?"

"Yes. You finally get your second lesson, Mr. Williams. You've been real patient."

"Hey, I never knew there was so much work involved in running an orchard. I thought you just let nature grow the apples, then picked them," he said, giving her a lopsided grin. "This has been educational, among other things."

Penny felt the heat rise on her face. "Wear sturdy—"

"Boots and long pants," Chris finished. "Yes, Teach, I remember." With a final pat to Rusty, he ambled off.

She watched him go with mixed feelings. Chris was certainly fun to be with. He was a friend she'd never had. But whatever was chewing on him was still there. It wasn't just the mountains he feared. It was something else. Underneath all his humor, she sensed determination and dread. Of what? Why was he so persistent about learning his way around these mountains? What was he looking for?

CHAPTER SEVEN

At Chris's insistence, they went on a wilderness hike ... no trails, just an objective.

When they reached Lookout Knob, Chris's face was grim and he was panting harder than Rusty. "It's no use, Penny. I'm never going to get the hang of this. I was hopelessly lost after the first half hour."

"Don't be so hard on yourself. It takes time to feel at home in the mountains."

"I don't have a lot of time."

"What's the rush? The mountains aren't going anywhere," Penny said, spreading some food on a flat boulder. "Sit and eat. You'll feel better."

Chris joined her, looking out over the acres and acres of trees, and shuddering. "I can't do it," he muttered under his breath.

"Do what?"

"Go to the top of Little River Gorge."

So that was it! He wanted to see the place where his uncle fell. Why didn't he just say so? "That's rough country up there. Besides, one side is posted private property."

"So the sheriff told me. I still want to go. Soon."

"Why?"

Chris deliberately filled his mouth with a sandwich and chewed.

Penny waited.

Finally, he swallowed and took a swig of water. "Okay. Uncle Pat said he found something up there. I want to see if it's still there."

Curiosity almost overcame her manners. She managed to curb it. "If it's that important, I can lead you. We're not too far from there now."

"No!" Chris's face was turning cherry red. "I mean—uh—it's illegal—posted. You might get in trouble. With the sheriff, I mean."

"Pretty lame, Chris," she said, shaking her head. "I'm already in trouble with our good sheriff."

Chris stood, jamming his hands into the back pockets of his jeans. "I know. I should go alone, though."

"It's up to you," she said, not wishing to push him. "See that gap between those two mountains? You go through there and are in Shady Valley. Climb the steepest rocky bluff and the gorge is directly below. Shouldn't take you more than an hour at most. Of course, if you want to go up the public side you have to cross the river first."

"He fell from this side," Chris mumbled. For a few minutes he said nothing else.

Penny sat quietly. Her fingers itched to draw him, standing in profile, gazing out over the mountains. Instead, she memorized every line—for later.

Chris seemed to be arguing with himself. Finally, he flashed his lopsided grin. "What the hey! I'm probably being a wimp. Let's do it."

Before he could change his mind, Penny packed up their gear and started off at a brisk pace.

"Since there's no point in my trying to figure out our

path, why don't I entertain you with a story," Chris offered after a few minutes.

"I like stories," Penny said.

"Okay. Let's see.... What do you know about Druids, Penny?"

"Nothing. Never heard of them."

"Well, this is a story about Druids. They were a very powerful religious group in Celtic Britain. They held sway long before the Romans and Christianity came. This story begins in Kidwelly, Wales...."

Sensing he didn't want her to look at him, Penny plunged ahead, listening hard. Chris was a good storyteller. His words drew pictures in her mind. She saw the white-robed priest—the girl on the altar—the flashing dagger—the blood spurting. A scream clogged her throat as the arrow flew. It took all her courage to keep walking as the story unfolded.

"On an April day in 1685, Padric set forth in search of Ian Cooper." Chris finished with an air of finality.

Penny whirled to face him. "You can't quit there! Did Padric find him? Did the Druid's curse work? What happened?"

His face white and drawn, Chris replied, "Padric found ample evidence in the Colonies that the curse worked, but he didn't find Ian or the Druid oak. His son Stephen found Ian Cooper's grave, though. But no one, from that day to this, has found the Druid oak ... and lived."

Penny shivered. "What an awful story!" Suddenly her mountains no longer felt friendly.

"Yeah, it's awesome," Chris said with a sheepish grin. "Kinda explains why the trees spook me, doesn't it? How far are we from the gorge?"

She searched his innocent-looking face. What was going on here? In spite of his offhand manner, she knew she'd heard fear and, yes, belief in his voice. "About twenty minutes," she replied, turning and going on.

Chris followed silently. But by the time they reached the posted barbed-wire fence, he was chatting normally again.

Penny slipped through the wires and held them apart for Chris and Rusty. She led Rusty to a thicket and ordered, "Stay. Guard." Then she turned to Chris. "He can warn us if one of the Dowdys comes along."

"We're not stealing anything. Why should these Dowdys care if I climb their rocks?"

"It's their land and it's rumored they may have a still or two on it. They're apt to shoot first and ask questions later. And just what do you mean by *I* climb their rocks?"

Chris put both hands on her shoulders and gazed down into her eyes. "Penny, you've been super. I couldn't have done this without you. But this is something I *have* to do alone. Okay?"

Her curiosity was no match for his pleading eyes. Reluctantly, she said, "All right, we'll wait here. Just watch your footing."

"Oh, I'll be supercautious. You can bank on that." With a confident smile he started up the slope.

Penny watched uneasily as he climbed around the boulders and scree. She wished he trusted her enough to tell her what was going on. She had the feeling he'd already told her more than he'd intended. Sinking down beside Rusty, she said, "We'll give him a half hour. If he's not back by then we're going after him."

Rusty nuzzled her hand comfortingly.

Time had almost run out when she heard Chris sliding down the slippery loose rocks. "Over here, Chris."

A dusty, bedraggled Chris joined her. "That didn't take long, did it?"

"You made good time." She saw unshed tears glistening in his eyes. "What's wrong?"

"Nothing. Any water left?" He collapsed in a heap by her side. After several long gulps, he wiped his mouth and tried for a smile. It didn't quite happen. "Guess I should be happy. There was nothing up there."

"What did you expect?"

A flush darkened Chris's sweaty face. "You might as well know what a fool I've been. I thought I might find the Druid oak. You know that story I told you? Well, Uncle Pat told it to me one night in the hospital. He said Padric Moore was our ancestor."

"Your uncle believed that tale?"

"Not when Grampa Moore first told it to him. Uncle Pat said he spent three years in research before he was convinced these journals and stuff were authentic. Then he found the Druid oak. Here. On this bluff."

It was too much. Penny found herself shaking her head vigorously. "It isn't possible. Did you believe him?"

Chris jumped to his feet and tried to dust himself off. "I don't know. I wanted to. My uncle was an intelligent man. A respected scholar. He said he had proof and a description of the tree. I didn't want to believe he'd lost his marbles. I wanted to check it out. So now I have. Let's get outta here."

Chris was hurting. She wanted to comfort him but didn't know how. "Maybe a blow on the head made him strange."

"Everything about this is strange! He believed this superstitious nonsense *before* he fell, Penny. Then he was recovering from the fall and *whammo*—he was wasting away from some mysterious something the doctors couldn't cure. We lost him, found him, and lost him again."

All she could say was, "I'm sorry, Chris."

"Thanks." He gave her a heartfelt smile. "You know, one of the reasons Mom and I decided to live up here was the caring people. Everyone was super to Uncle Pat. Would you believe he had lots of Glyn Ayr visitors when he was in the hospital? Members of the Rescue Squad, neighbors, preachers, anyone who was visiting the hospital—all stopped by to visit a man they hardly knew. It sure made a difference when Mom and I couldn't be around."

"That's just the mountain way. Nothing special."

"It was special to us," Chris said. "And much appreciated."

Noting how tired and depressed Chris was, Penny angled them toward Route 5, hoping to snag a ride with someone she knew. Just as they reached the highway, a white Cadillac came around the bend. She threw up her hand to flag it down, but the car sped on by.

"Who was that?" Chris asked, seeing her frown.

"Pastor Cawper. He could've given us a lift," Penny said, lowering her arm.

"Cawper? I think he was one of the preachers who visited Uncle Pat. It's a name I'd never heard before."

"I don't doubt he visited. Preacher Cawper's everywhere. He's always trying to drum up new members for that little offbeat church of his. He won't get far by being snobby."

"Maybe he didn't want dog hair in his new car."

"Maybe. I call it downright un-neighborly not to help folks when they need it."

"Don't get hyper on my account, Penny. I've got another mile or two left in me."

"Never thought you didn't," she replied, surprised that he'd known what she was doing.

"Then let's can the gloom and doom. We should be

happy to be out on such a great day. No evil menace is lurking in the woods either."

A horn tootled behind them. "Want a ride into town?"

"Sure, Andrew," Penny said, smiling at the leader of the Shady Valley commune. "We're plumb tuckered. This is Chris Williams."

"Howdy, Chris. Hop in the back, if you can find a spot. Me and Big John here are heading to the hardware store. Pump broke again."

Penny waved to the other figure in the cab, and all three of them piled into the truck. By the time they reached Glyn Ayr, Chris was smiling cheerfully again. "Come on," he said, helping Penny from the truck bed. "Let's celebrate with a burger and fries. My treat."

"Thanks, Andrew," Penny called. "We'd better not, Chris. It's getting late."

"Please? It's the least I can do for my teach. You'd like a big, juicy burger, wouldn't you, Rusty?"

"*Woof,*" Rusty agreed, tail wagging.

"He can't go inside."

"So we'll get carry out. Look, those tables will be perfect."

Laughing, she agreed. Although she felt conspicuous sitting at an outdoor table, it was worth it to see Chris so happy. She knew it must be awful to know someone you loved and admired was demented. Still, it was better than believing in that gruesome story!

Chris returned with a loaded tray. They'd just polished off the last scrap when a shadow darkened their table. Penny looked up. Big John hovered over them. A stone disk dangled from one giant paw. "This belong to one of you? Andrew found it in the truck bed."

"It's mine," Chris said, grabbing the object. "Guess the chain broke. Thanks."

"Welcome," Big John said, lumbering away.

Chris tried to stash the object away before Penny got a good look at it.

Penny raised a questioning eyebrow. "What is it?"

Reluctantly, Chris put the smooth stone on the table. "A Celtic cross. Uncle Pat was wearing it when he fell."

Gingerly, Penny traced the cross with her finger. It felt warm. "It's beautiful," she murmured. "Father Stephen's?"

Chris shrugged. "So Uncle Pat said."

"This was part of the proof?"

"The only part I can find! I've turned our place upside down and haven't come across any journals or the research Uncle Pat claimed to have done. Zip. Nada. Nothing. Today was my last shot. I was sure I'd find proof up there. Well, it's over, Penny. Finished. Done. Okay?"

Penny let out a sigh of relief. "Good. I think that's smart, Chris."

"Yeah, me, too," he said, slipping the cross into a pocket. "Let me dump our trash and I'll walk you home."

"You'll do no such thing! It's wasted effort. Rusty and I will cut across Bramson woods and be home almost by the time you are."

"Things will be different when I get my driver's license in a year or so," Chris said.

"Maybe not," Penny teased. "Maybe you won't like dog hairs in your car."

Chris grinned. "Dog hair won't hurt Uncle Pat's jeep. And Mom says the jeep's mine when I get licensed."

"Then no more hiking for you, huh?" Penny said. "Thanks for the treat, Chris."

"My pleasure. Thank *you* for putting up with my wild ghost chase."

A group of kids came between them as they left the

patio. A sick feeling engulfed Penny when Ina Mae trilled, "Hi, Chris. Come help me celebrate. I just got a big paycheck."

"Congratulations. Penny and I were just leaving."

"Oh, she won't mind," Ina Mae said, dismissing Penny with a wave of her hand. "This is a high school thing."

"Penny may not mind but I would," Chris shot back. "See, rudeness always makes me want to puke."

A ripple of laughter ran through the group. Ina Mae did not join in. "Suit yourself," she said and flounced off.

The rest of the group followed her, looking embarrassed.

This exchange happened so quickly that Penny didn't have time to say a word.

"What's with Miss Congeniality?" Chris asked as they walked off.

"Ina Mae was promoted every year. She doesn't like dummies."

"Jeez, you're ten times smarter than that airhead. Can I call you tomorrow?"

So this wasn't the end! A smile made Penny's face glow. "Better make it after one. We should be finished with Sunday dinner by then."

"You got it."

Penny went home feeling more satisfied with herself than she'd ever felt. Wasn't it strange that having one person—outside of your family—believing in you made such a difference? Chris liked her! Wanted to be with her, in spite of the fact that she was dyslexic. Now that the mystery about his uncle was solved, that tiny unhappy frown on Chris's face would disappear. Sure, it was sad that the Moores had been chasing smoke all these years. But it was over. Finished. Done. Just like Chris said.

" 'God's in his heaven. All's right with the world,' " she said to Rusty.

CHAPTER EIGHT

October

She should have been happy. This October was picture-perfect. The mountains were ablaze with trees of red, gold, and orange. The air was perfumed with wood smoke, apples, and fallen leaves. Images flowed easily onto her sketch pad. Except for that one stubborn glen that didn't want to be painted. She and Chris spent as much time as possible together. Even school wasn't such a pain. Not that reading was any easier, but the new teacher, Miss Longacre, didn't treat her like a retard. Sheriff Peale had stopped bothering her. So why was she uneasy?

Examining her feelings, Penny changed out of her Sunday clothes into jeans. Tying her hair in a ponytail, she made a face at the image in the mirror. Uncle Arly's nose was to blame! He still insisted he smelled brimstone, a sure sign that the Evil was about. Poor old fellow! He was so worried he didn't want her to bring him his supper anymore. Every night she had to reassure him that everything was fine. Thank goodness, she hadn't told him Chris's weird story about the Druid curse. Uncle Arly really would be upset. To tell the truth, that story still bothered her at times. Somehow it just wouldn't go away.

"You," she said, pointing a finger at her image, "had better shape up. Your imagination's running wild."

"Penny!" A voice interrupted her thoughts. "Dinner's on the table."

"Coming, Aunt Martha," she said, running downstairs.

Several times during the meal, Penny caught her uncle staring at her. When he finally pushed back from the table, he said, "You been looking a tad peaked lately. You comin' down with something?"

Penny smiled and tried to look healthy. "No, sir. I'm just fine."

"I noticed it, too," Martha said. "Lord knows, I never thought I'd say this, but maybe you oughta take some time to yourself. You haven't been out on your lonesome for quite a while. You're as edgy as a cat on hot bricks."

"Reckon I don't like my own company as much as I used to," Penny admitted.

"Couldn't be a certain good-looking young man, could it?" Jake said, teasingly.

"No way! Chris and I are just friends."

Martha kept watching Penny as she cleared the table. "Honey, why don't you take the day off? Go for a stroll in the woods by yourself. I'll run the stand today."

"No-siree-bob! It's my turn. You and Uncle Jake deserve your day off."

"Can't argue with that," Jake said, stretching contentedly.

"I can!" Martha retorted. "I don't think we ought to be open on Sundays anyways."

"Now, Martha . . ." began Jake.

"Whoa!" Penny said. "Before y'all chew that old bone again, I need the cash box. Think Ernesto has the apples ready, Uncle Jake?"

"He said he'd stock up the stand soon as they got back from Mass. Should be ready when you get down there."

"I'll take Uncle Arly his Sunday dinner," Martha said. "You run along and get set up."

"Okay. But don't pay any attention to his nose," Penny warned. She collected the money box and Rusty and went down to the roadside stand where people were already waiting.

Sunday trade was brisk. Despite Martha's objection, Penny knew it was good business to be open on Sunday. Leaf-lookers and locals by the dozens followed the signs to Fox Hollow Orchards. She was busier than a one-armed banjo picker.

Her heart began hammering when she saw the familiar brown cruiser pull up. Its normal rhythm quickly returned when Deputy Coombs climbed out.

"Afternoon, Penny. You got any apples left?"

"Rusty and I saved the best just for you. What'll it be?"

"A bushel of Yorks and a bushel of each kind of Delicious. I reckon you been good lately, huh?" he said, patting Rusty's head.

"He's always good! Can he help it if Miz Parker's chickens peck on him?"

When Deputy Coombs chuckled his whole large belly shook. He looked like a big, brown Santa Claus. "Yeah, them banty chickens is a b-i-g danger to a small dog like Rusty."

"Speaking of danger," Penny said, "anything new about Melissa?"

All the laughter disappeared from the deputy's face. "We know a tad more. Sheriff's keepin' it quiet, but he reckons it was one o' them rit-u-al murders."

"What's that mean?"

"Means some kinda ceremony was carried out on Melissa. She was bashed on the head three times, stabbed, and choked by a leather thong. Any one of them things coulda killed her. But the medical examiner said they was done *after* she was dead! Lordy, that was one gruesome report!'' He wiped his round face with a big handkerchief. ''Now don't you let on I told you any of this.''

A sour, metalic taste rose in Penny's throat. She swallowed hard. ''Why would someone do such awful things?''

''I don't know. Guess we wouldn't have had that much to go on if that ole limestone hadn't caved in exposin' her body.''

An icy finger of fear ran down Penny's spine. She couldn't stop the shiver that shook her.

''Hey, now! Don't you fret,'' Deputy Coombs said. ''We'll get this killer. Sheriff's onto something. He's smarter'n folks give him credit for.''

''I sure hope so,'' Penny said as two other cars pulled up. She took the deputy's money and moved off to help her new customers.

Looking as if he regretted his loose tongue, Deputy Coombs loaded his apples into the cruiser and took off.

A steady stream of customers kept Penny from thinking about Deputy Coombs's revelations. But by 4:30 traffic had slowed to a mere trickle. She had begun to close up when a splotchy, once-red truck chugged up. ''Hi, Turkey,'' Penny called, smiling. ''Haven't seen you in a month of Sundays.''

A man loped toward her with a happy grin splitting his long, craggy face. ''You're a sight for sore eyes, Penny Brown.'' The protruding Adam's apple that earned him his name bobbed merrily on his sun-reddened neck. ''How ya been? How's Martha and Jake?''

''We're right as rain. Been a good harvest. Congratulations, Mr. Turkey Collins! I heard you took top honors again at the Fiddler's Convention in Galax.''

Turkey looked modestly at the toes of his scuffed boots. "Yep. You heard right."

"You're gonna have to build another room at your place to hold all your trophies and ribbons!"

"Been too busy buildin' for other folks to do any o' my own. Work keeps me on the trot. I could've used two o' me, 'cept the wife says one ugly geezer's all she can tolerate," Turkey said, eyes twinkling. "Hear you been busy, too."

"Me?"

"Uh-huh. Heard you been sparkin' that new boy lives on River Road."

Penny tried in vain to keep her face from flushing. "Grapevine over to Jordan Mountain must be outta whack. I'm not sparking anyone! Chris and I are friends, that's all."

Turkey nodded solemnly. "Bein' friends helps a heap. Good way to start. Sure was sorry t' hear about that boy's uncle. Dr. Moore, he was a nice feller. Not one bit uppity, like some o' them college professors."

"I figured you did his remodeling!"

"Aye-ya. Dr. Moore, he was right particular 'bout what he wanted done."

"Uh-oh! Fussy, was he? I better hear about this. Could run in the family."

"Apple don't fall far from the tree, for sure. Well, I don't think you got much to worry on. Dr. Moore was kerful but not picky. Had a bee in his bonnet over something, but he warn't tetched. All told, I'd say he was a serious, smart, dignified feller. 'Cept onct," Turkey said, laughing.

"What happened?"

"When I showed him that secret room he whooped and hollered like a young'un on Christmas mornin'. He even done a little jig 'round the room. Funniest sight I ever laid eyes on."

Penny was too surprised to speak.

"Said he allus wanted a secret room," Turkey continued. "Ast me not to let on to anybody about it. But I reckon it's okay now he's gone."

"Oh, yes," Penny said, finding her voice. "The Williamses should know. Where is this room, Turkey?"

"In the liberry. See, the more I studied on it, the more I knowed that room was out of true. So I commenced pokin' around. Lo and behold, that back bookshelf swung out! Scared the pure, livin' fire outta me. Thought I'd broke somethin'. But there it were. This musty little room just a sittin' there."

"And you showed Dr. Moore?"

"Yep. After he got over his fit, he ast me to run the air-conditionin' in there, too. Said it would make a perfect private office."

That was why Chris couldn't find his uncle's papers! Penny thought. Or his proof of the Druid oak. The idea sent a chill through her. She shivered and tried to hide it.

Turkey didn't notice. "It's a good hidey-hole. I come across a few sich rooms a'fore. None as good a work as this one, though."

"I think we ought to keep it a secret, then. Just in case the Williamses want to use it or something."

"Mum's the word," Turkey promised as Jake's pickup truck rumbled up. "I'll take a few o' these apples off'n your hands 'fore you pack it in."

Penny was so nervous she hardly remembered saying good-bye to Turkey or closing the stand.

"You wanna ride back to the house?"

"What? Oh, no thanks, Ernesto. I'll walk."

"You okay, Miss Penny? Somebody make you mad? Hurt your feelings?"

"No, Ernesto. I just have some thinking to do. I'm fine. Really." She tried to smile for the small, happy man.

"You go on then. I finish here."

Penny took the cash box and walked slowly up the lane. What Deputy Coombs had told her was almost too horrible to think about. The pictures it drew in her mind were sickening. She closed her eyes, but the pictures remained. Why? Why would anyone do those things to a dead body? Was the deputy right? Was Sheriff Peale smart or was it all bluster?

The secret room was another matter. Should she tell Chris? Lately, he seemed to have forgotten his uncle's weird story. What if there were papers and stuff in the room that brought back all the pain and worry?

"I don't know what to do, Rusty. Maybe I should leave well enough alone. I never heard of these Druids. I bet nobody else ever did either. It's just a scary story somebody dreamed up. Right?"

Rusty leaned against her leg, rumbling in the way Penny swore was talking.

Penny rubbed his ears affectionately. He'd been sticking beside her like glue lately. Aunt Martha said he had purple fits when she didn't get off the school bus. He'd even begun sleeping underneath her window at night, instead of in his doghouse.

"You'll always protect me, won't you, boy?" she said, bending and cradling his head in her hands.

Rusty looked at her, his big brown eyes pleading. "*Ar-r-ar-ar,*" he ruffed again.

Penny kissed the top of his head. "I know you're trying to tell me something. I only wish I was smart enough to understand you. Maybe you could tell me what to do. I think I'll just wait until it feels right before I tell Chris anything. That sound okay to you, boy?"

CHAPTER NINE

"What?" Chris shouted as they approached the special Harvest Fest bus.

"Turkey Collins told me about it last Sunday," Penny explained. "I thought you might want to find it before we went over to the Harvest Fest. There's another bus at two."

"You bet I do! Jeez, Louise, a secret room! Why didn't you tell me sooner?"

"I didn't want to tell you over a party line." This wasn't strictly the truth. She hadn't wanted to tell him at all. But, somehow, something kept nagging at her ... forcing her.

"Do you mind missing a little of the festival? Now's a perfect time to investigate. Mom's gone down to Roanoke College for the day."

"I don't mind," she lied. She was scared to death of what they'd find. All week her head and her heart had played tug-of-war. Her head told her a supernatural, killer tree was impossible! Her heart said Dr. Moore's story was important to Chris, therefore, important to her. Heart won over head.

Chris grabbed her hand and made a mad dash up River Road. "Come on," he urged.

"What's your hurry? The room isn't going anywhere."

"Today's October twenty-fourth, in case you forgot," he snapped, unlocking the front door.

"So?"

"So next Saturday's All Hallows' eve."

The tone of his voice left no doubt. Chris believed the Druid oak existed! With dragging steps, she followed him down the hall to the library.

"Which bookcase?"

"Turkey said the back one. I guess he meant toward the back of the house." Penny stepped tentatively into the room. All these books! They made her even more nervous.

Chris was already exploring the shelves.

Penny hung back. "Why didn't your uncle tell you about this place?"

"Because he had no idea we'd come here to live. Mom didn't tell him about the divorce. Afraid to upset him."

"Why'd he tell you about the Druid oak and not your mother?"

Chris finished one section and moved to another. "Jeez! I don't know, Penny. Guess he didn't want to upset *her*. I think he had to confess his failure to somebody. I was available."

"But he didn't ask you to keep on with his task, did he?"

"No, he—Eureka!" Chris yelled as his finger found a button.

A whole section of the bookcase swung slowly outward.

Chris reached for her hand and they stepped into the darkness. With his free hand, Chris felt for a light switch. Suddenly the area was flooded with bright fluorescent lights.

The room was sparsely furnished: a long table with a stack of newspaper clippings and a computer, a few books on a bookrack, a swivel chair, and a battered wooden chest.

The wall behind the table had an enlarged map of the United States. A line of black pins wove through the Atlantic states.

Chris was the first to move. "Let's see what's on the computer."

With every nerve in her body tingling, Penny stood still, absorbing the feel of the place. The air seemed hushed, almost like the sanctuary of a church. While Chris fiddled with the machine, mumbling to himself, she went slowly over to the map. The line that curled from Massachusetts to Virginia reminded her of a snake. Each shiny cluster of three pins looked like the diamonds of a mountain rattler. Shuddering, she turned away. "Find anything?"

"Just the usual stuff. He must have had a coded file," Chris answered without taking his eyes from the screen. "Look through those newspapers and books and see what you find."

Books? Newspapers? He wanted *her* to go through those? Shaking her head, she began thumbing through the stack of papers. At first the letters did their usual tricks, scrambling themselves all over the pages. But by concentrating, she managed to make them behave. After a few minutes, she wished she hadn't. The articles, clipped in sets of threes, were from Pennsylvania, West Virginia, Maryland, and Virginia. All concerned missing girls! Some were several years old. Some recent. A single small item had a picture, under which were the words: "HAVE YOU SEEN THIS GIRL? Tanya Blevins of Shady Valley reported missing on November 3, 1990." Penny dropped the paper as if it were blazing. "Oh, oh, oh!"

Chris was by her side in a flash. "What?"

Wordlessly, Penny pointed.

Chris went through the material much faster than she. "Always three," he said in a hollow voice. "Except this one. I wonder why?"

"Melissa could have been number two," Penny mumbled, turning to stare at the map where only one pin rested.

"Jeez, Louise! This is unreal!"

"The newspaper articles are real," she pointed out. "Your uncle didn't invent those."

"No, but I've read statistics about thousands of girls who run away from home each year. That doesn't mean they were victims of the Druid's curse."

"True," she agreed. The hairs on the back of her neck were prickling uncomfortably. The room suddenly seemed twenty degrees colder.

"There has to be more. This isn't proof of anything," Chris said, plopping back in front of the computer. "See what you can find in those books."

Penny looked at the assorted volumes, each decorated with a confetti of white markers, and sighed. "I'll get a chair." Chris didn't respond. He was totally absorbed as his fingers flew over the keyboard.

Rubbing the goosebumps on her arms, Penny went back into the library. This room felt warmer, more normal. Photographs, plaques, and pictures decorated the walls not covered by bookcases. Stalling, she walked around looking at the photographs. Most were of Chris, his mother, and a look-alike man that had to be Dr. Moore. Penny chuckled at one picture where a short, scrawny, snaggle-toothed Chris proudly held up an equally scrawny fish. So Chris wasn't always tall and handsome! He sure was a carbon copy of his mom and uncle now, though. Feeling guilty, she grabbed a straight-back chair from under a picture of a fierce red dragon and went back to her assigned task.

Chris evidently hadn't missed her. He was busily tapping keys and swearing under his breath when the machine beeped at him again and again.

Penny settled down with the smallest of the books and tried to read the marked passages. It was slow work. She was concentrating deeply when a loud crash caused her to jump, dropping the book to the floor.

"Sorry," Chris said, rubbing his hand. "I took out my anger on the table. I can't get in, Penny. I've tried every password I can think of: Druid, Wales, Moore, Celtic, Father Stephen, Padric. No go!"

The words popped into her head from nowhere. "Try 'red dragon.'"

"The national symbol of Wales?"

Penny's mouth hung open, but no words came out. Where had that idea come from?

Not waiting for an answer, Chris typed furiously and pressed the Enter key. The blank screen filled with writing. "Yes!" he shouted. "Good work, Watson!"

"What does it say?"

Chris scrolled through the material. "It's a big file. First is the story Grampa Moore told Uncle Pat. Ah, now we're cooking!"

"Read it!"

"'Research procedures into the matter of the Druid curse,'" he read. A smile played on his lips. "Once a professor, always a professor."

"Go on," Penny begged.

"He outlines every step he took, from authenticating the age of the journals to tracing clusters of three missing girls," Chris answered, scanning the text slowly.

An icy shiver ran through Penny as she glanced at the

black line snaking its way into her beloved mountains. "So he came to believe this awful tale?"

Chris began reading. " 'Few educated people believe with Hamlet that there are more things in heaven and earth than are dreamt of in our philosophy. Today there is no belief in ghosts, curses, or ancient magic. In fact, no one believes Evil exists.' "

"Uncle Arly does," Penny murmured.

"What?"

"Nothing. Keep going."

" 'I could not support my ancestors' delusions,' " Chris continued, " 'until I read the journals and researched the matter for three years. My conclusion: The Druid oak exists. The spirit of that ancient, powerful Druid lives. And each All Hallows' eve, from dusk until dawn, the Druid oak moves about the land claiming a human sacrifice. There are usually three victims in an area before the Druid moves on. This cluster pattern made documentation easier. According to my research, the Druid oak has progressed from Massachusetts to Virginia's Blue Ridge.' "

Penny's eyes went to the snakey line on the large map. "Here. Right here."

Chris gave a brief nod and continued reading. " 'I had the means of destroying the Druid oak, the scroll. My father died before giving me the translation. But, fortunately, I have a friend, Dr. Owen Jones at the University of Wales in Aberystwyth, who is an expert on Druids and the Celtic language. I sent him the scroll, which he says is in Q-Celtic, the secret, priestly language of the Druids. Owen has given me the pronunciation and intonation by phone. Time is of the essence. I am the last Seeker.' "

With one accord, they jumped up and headed for the small trunk. Chris pryed open the tight lid. Ledgers and tablets of various sizes and ages were neatly stacked inside.

"Where's the scroll?" Penny asked as he carefully removed each labeled item.

"It's not here," Chris replied, sitting back on his heels.

"You think this Dr. Jones may still have it?"

He helped her to her feet, shaking his head. "I don't know. Let's see if it's in the computer. We're dead in the water without it."

Chris plunked himself before the screen and Penny went back to the book she'd been reading. A sudden gust of air turned the pages. Penny looked down and yelled, "Chris!"

CHAPTER TEN

Even with Chris holding her, she was shaking. "That's what I s-saw on Big Bear," she said, pointing to some strange lines. "Th-those marks were carved in a stone."

Chris examined the page. " 'Ogham script. The only known form of Druidic writing is made by cutting notches along the edges of stones. Generally used for writing epitaphs or marking gravesites.' " He frowned at her. "You actually saw marks like these? Did you tell Sheriff Peale?"

"I saw them, but I didn't think the sheriff would be interested in some old scratches on rocks. Should we go tell him now?"

"You think he'd believe any of this?" Chris asked, waving his arms around.

Penny shook her head. In a small voice she said, "No, *I* didn't believe it . . . until now."

"Sit down," Chris ordered. "You're white as a ghost. I'll get you some water."

"No!" Penny cried. She didn't want to be alone in this room. "I'm okay. Oh, Chris, what are we going to do?"

Chris's face looked carved from granite. "We'll get to

the bottom of this." He strode back to the computer. "Let's see what else Uncle Pat has to say."

Aloud, he read the summary of the journals. They told a dark tale of evil, of frustration, and of death. Only Nathaniel Moore, in 1890, actually described the Druid oak: an enormous, spreading tree with a crown of mistletoe. No birds nest in its branches. It bears no acorns. No living thing grows under its limbs.

Nathaniel's words took shape in Penny's mind. She could see the tree. Feel its evil. It was . . .

"Jeez! You look ready to pass out," Chris cried in alarm.

The vision vanished. Penny shook herself. "Go on. Read the rest."

"There isn't much more. Uncle Pat had some theory he wanted to check out with Dr. Jones."

"What kind of theory?"

"He doesn't say. The last entry is dated October seventh." Sadness filled his voice as he read. " 'Late this afternoon while looking through my binoculars, I found the Druid oak. The discovery is both a relief and a terror. The prince of Denmark's words again come to mind: "Time is out of joint: O cused spite, that ever I was born to set it right!" But I was born and I am the last Moore. The task is mine.

" 'Haven't heard from Owen concerning my theory. I can't reach him by phone tonight. However, I have been extremely careful. I foresee no danger. In all probability, I was wrong anyway.

" 'God willing, tomorrow I will put an end to this Druid curse.' "

In the silence that followed, Penny could hear her own heart beating. She was filled with fear and pity. Fear of this monstrous evil. Pity for the man who'd given up his profession, his time, and his life to end the horrible sacrifices.

Chris coughed, breaking into her thoughts. "That's it. Uncle Pat fell the next day."

"He was climbing the posted side of the gorge."

Nodding, Chris said, "I think he saw the oak from the public overlook. All I know is that it wasn't there when I went up. There wasn't an oak of any size. Just a few scrub trees and some pines."

"Where did it go?"

"Beats me. I guess it's hiding somewhere among these thousands and thousands of trees. What better place to hide a tree than in a forest?" Chris's voice was bitter and without hope.

Again, a soft breeze touched Penny's cheek. "Call Dr. Jones."

"In Wales?"

"The University of Wales in Aberystwyth," Penny repeated from memory.

"Right," Chris said, looking at his watch. "It's four-thirty here. What time is it in Wales? Jeez! Four-thirty? We've been here all afternoon! Mom'll be home any minute. Let's get outta here."

"What about the phone call?"

"No one will be at a university on a weekend. Besides, I have to find his number." He grabbed a stack of books and urged her toward the opening. "Will you help me go through these?"

"I won't be much help," she said looking at the books with alarm.

"Penny, I know it isn't easy for you, but you read today. More importantly, you make connections that are out of my reach. I need you. You can do it."

She saw the confidence in his eyes. He was right. She

could read if she put forth the effort, just like that reading specialist said. Only she hadn't wanted to do the exercises or practice. Reading hadn't seemed important. Not for an artist. Not for a solitary who was quitting school as soon as the law allowed. Penny extended her hands for the books.

Chris put the books in her hands and then, surprising both of them, brushed his lips on hers. The kiss was feather-light, but Penny felt it clear down to her toes. "You're something else, Penelope Brown."

Before Penny could say a word, a voice called, "Chris, I'm home!"

Glancing quickly at the bookcase, Chris called, "We're in the library, Mom."

With a click of high heels, Mrs. Williams came down the hall. "Too bad your festival was rained out. Did you get to enjoy any of it?"

Penny and Chris looked at each other with surprise. Enclosed in the secret chamber, they hadn't known it was raining. "No," they answered in unison. Penny hoped her face wasn't as red as it felt.

However, Chris was as cool as a cucumber. "Got your books, Penny? I was just going to walk her home, Mom."

"All right. I'll get out of these fancy duds and fix us some dinner," Mrs. Williams said. A wide smile lit her face. "You two didn't eat me out of house and home, did you?"

They shook their heads. For once, they hadn't eaten anything. Chris's stomach growled at the mention of food.

"No matter. I bought T-bone steaks to celebrate," Mrs. Williams said. Her eyes danced merrily.

"Wow! What's the occasion?"

"I have a job interview at Roanoke College Tuesday morning! The professor who teaches all the Shakespeare courses has to take an emergency leave."

"Hey, that's your bag, Mom!"

"There's certainly something to be said for being in the right place at the right time. I was getting awfully tired of doing these book reviews. Hurry back, Chris. Suddenly I'm starved."

"Me, too," Chris said over a ferocious stomach rumble. "I'll be back shortly."

The interlude with Mrs. Williams lightened Penny's mood. Somehow, she felt as if the afternoon's terror had been a bad dream. She was awake now. Only the memory of the kiss lingered.

"I'm sorry we missed the festival," Chris said as they stopped at her door.

"That's okay," she said, dreamily.

"I hope I can find Uncle Pat's address book," he said, bringing back the horror. "I don't know when to call without Mom knowing. She'll go ballistic if she finds out what we're doing."

Penny chose her words carefully. "If you mean she won't like it, maybe she's right. Think about it. Why make an expensive phone call when we don't know where the Druid oak is?"

"I want to talk to this Dr. Jones," Chris replied, looking stubborn. "I owe it to Uncle Pat."

She had seen that same look on Uncle Jake's face. No use arguing with it. "Then call while your mother's at the job interview."

"Yeah. Excellent idea. I could cut class and come home. Think you could get away, too?"

In for a penny, in for a pound, she thought. "Sure. What time?"

"I'll find out when Mom's leaving and call you. Or better yet, I'll come over tomorrow and we can plan this out."

Penny shook her head regretfully. "We're having a bunch of relatives in from Galax tomorrow after church. They only come over once a year. I'll be expected to hang around."

"Will you have time to read any of the books?"

"I'll do the best I can. What am I looking for exactly?"

Chris shrugged. "Beats me. Anything that ties in—like that ogham script—I guess. The more we know, the better. I'll read my stack, too. We can consult on the phone."

"Be careful what you say," Penny warned. "We're on a party line."

"Thanks for the tip. I'll watch it," Chris said, leaning toward her.

Thinking he might kiss her again, Penny opened the door quickly. Not that she didn't want him to. But she was afraid Martha or Jake might be watching. "Call me after six tomorrow, okay?"

With a lopsided grin, replied, "You got it."

The grandfather clock struck half after the hour as Penny walked inside.

"That you, Penny?" Martha called.

"We been waitin' on you like pigs at the trough," Uncle Jake yelled.

"It's me. I'll be right down." She scurried to her room to put away the books. They'd ask a million questions if they saw what she had. Books and Penny were usually like oil and water.

After a hasty meal, Penny and Rusty set out on the nightly trip to Uncle Arly's. It was a relief to be alone for a few minutes. The rain had stopped and the evening was crisp and clear.

Her thoughts were anything but clear. Could she really believe Dr. Moore's tale? Was there such a thing as a three-hundred-year-old curse? Yet Tanya was missing and

Melissa was dead. And then there were those strange marks she'd seen. Did it all fit together somehow? Even if it did, what could she and Chris possibly do to end these unholy sacrifices?

Adding to her confusion was the kiss. She had no experience in such matters. Was the intense, delicious warmth that flowed through her normal? How would it feel if he really kissed her, like people did on some of those television shows? The mere thought made her warm and weak-kneed.

Face flushed, she stepped up onto Uncle Arly's porch and tried the doorknob. It was locked! "Open up, Uncle Arly. Your supper's here."

Shuffling steps came toward the door. "That you, Penny?"

"Sure is. Me, pork roast, mashed potatoes, and peas."

The door creaked open just a slit. Uncle Arly peered through the crack. "What you been up to, gal?"

His question deepened the flush on her face. "Nothing much. Harvest festival was rained out."

"Not what I meant a'tall," he grumbled, stumping back to his chair by the fire.

Penny carried his tray to a table beside the chair. Something about her old friend sent a shiver of alarm racing through her. "Why'd you have the door locked, Uncle Arly?"

He sat heavily in the rocker. His gnarly hand reached out for her. "I reckon you think I be plumb tetched, but I know what I know. Devil's been walkin' and watchin', Penny. I smelled 'im! You best go kerful."

Penny patted his hand. "Don't fret about me, Uncle Arly. I have Rusty. He'll chase any devils away. How's your rheumatiz? That new medicine doing you any good?"

Talking about his aches and pains distracted Uncle Arly.

As soon as he finished eating, Penny gathered the plates and tray and left. Once outside, she couldn't help taking a deep sniff of air. All she smelled was the wood smoke from Uncle Arly's fire! Laughing uneasily, she and Rusty started home.

In the distance she heard a car engine start up. Probably some courting couple pulled off down by Peak Creek, she thought. Her lips tingled with the memory of Chris's kiss.

Chapter Eleven

"Owen Jones here."

Chris swallowed nervously at the sound of the very clipped voice. "Dr. Jones, this is Chris Williams in Glyn Ayr, Virginia. I'm Patrick Moore's nephew."

There was a brief pause. "Yes, Patrick often spoke of you, Christopher. I was sorry to hear of your uncle's death. How may I be of assistance?"

"Well . . . you see, Mom and I moved here after Uncle Pat died. I—I've found some of his research notes and they—uh—mention your name."

"Yes, Patrick and I consulted on a few matters."

"Would you happen to have the scroll?" blurted Chris.

This time the pause was longer. "May I ask why?"

"Two girls are missing. Well, one girl's still missing. The other one's body was found in a grave marked by an inscription in ogham."

"I see. Perhaps I can locate the document in question. May I return your call?"

"Sure. The number is—"

"I have Patrick's number," Dr. Jones replied briskly. "Unless it has been changed."

"No, sir, it's the same number."

The line went dead. Chris put down the receiver and wiped his sweaty hand on his jeans. "Jeez, that guy's weird."

Penny hung up the extension phone. "No, I think he's just being cautious. I think he was afraid you weren't who you said you were."

"How could you tell that from those few words he grudgingly gave out? What a jerk!" Chris paced the library, chewing on his lower lip. When the phone finally rang, he snatched up the receiver and practically shouted, "Hello."

"May I speak with Christopher Williams?"

"Yes, Dr. Jones. This is Chris Williams."

"I have the document in question in front of me. What would you like to know?"

A sigh of relief escaped from Penny's throat.

"Is there someone else on the line?" Dr. Jones demanded.

"It's Penelope Brown, Dr. Jones. I found some ogham script on a rock. Chris and I are working on this together," Penny said quickly.

"I'm wearing a stone cross," Chris added in desperation. "Could you read the scroll to us?"

"Ah, yes. Patrick's four-pointed talisman," Dr. Jones said. "I remember it well."

"Not well enough," Chris retorted. "This is a Celtic cross in a circle."

This time the sigh came from the other side of the Atlantic. "Very well. The document reads as follows: 'For this outrage you shall pay. I commit my spirit into this oak. As long as one piece remains, I shall live. From dusk until dawn on All Hallows' eve I shall roam the land, claiming my blood sacrifice.'"

Penny moaned.

"Is this the curse Father Stephen heard and believed?" Chris asked with doubt evident in his voice.

"We were closer to the old ways then," Dr. Jones said mildly. "There's more. At great peril to himself and his faith, Father Stephen obtained the method for ending the curse. Patrick memorized it. I doubt it would mean very much to you."

"Would you read it anyway?" Chris asked. His finger hovered over a button on the answering machine. "And is it okay if I record it?"

"Good heavens! Have you found the object in question?"

"No, sir. We want to be ready if we do."

"You are dabbling with ancient, dangerous forces. Your uncle—were he alive—would attest to that," Dr. Jones warned.

"We know," Penny said, ignoring the icy chill running up her spine.

"Very well," Dr. Jones said after a long pause. "Are you ready?"

Chris pressed the button. "Go ahead, Dr. Jones."

In a somber voice, Dr. Jones began. " 'With a staff of ash draw the holy circle around the outer edge of the tree. Once the circle is complete, it must not be penetrated. Seal the holy circle by walking three times around it, repeating: *"Athair, Oregetoria, Catumoros! Arglwydd orwai trawy'r anialwch. Sygn traws.* Amen." Stay and watch until the spell be broken.' "

"Jeez!"

"Precisely. Christopher, this is very dangerous ground you two are treading. My advice is that you forget what you've heard. Next year I plan to take a sabbatical and come to the United States. I would like to continue your uncle's research. Would that be agreeable?"

"Sure. I'd like to meet you. And don't worry. We don't have anything to draw a circle around," Chris said. "Thanks for talking—"

"Dr. Jones," Penny interjected, "what was this theory Dr. Moore wrote you about?"

"That is precisely why this is dangerous, Miss Brown," Dr. Jones replied. "After studying all the journals Patrick wondered if Ian Cooper's appearance on the scene was accidental. You see, we now know there were three orders of Druids: bards, vates, and priests. Patrick theorized that Ian Cooper was a vate, sent to serve and protect the Druid priest."

"So?" Chris asked, frowning into the phone.

"Patrick wondered if Ian Cooper's tombstone had given the Moores a false sense of security. What if Ian Cooper had passed *his* task along to *his* sons, just as the Moores had done? Could a vate still be protecting this priest? It would certainly explain the untimely deaths of any Moore who came close to discovering the whereabouts of this tree. It is a viable theory, though I never was able to confirm it for Patrick."

The cold surrounding Penny intensified. Something whispered wordlessly, *This is the truth.*

Penny didn't hear the rest of what Chris said, but she saw him put down the receiver.

Chris came over and took the extension phone from her hand. "Pretty weird, huh? Guess there's nothing we can do but wait until next year. You don't know of any Coopers around, do you?"

"No. Not unless it's someone at the commune. They go by only their first names."

The hopelessness of their situation hit them both at the

same time. Tears of frustration welled in Chris's eyes but remained unshed. He removed the tape from the answering machine and inserted another one. "I'll keep this in my room, just in case we stumble on something in the next year."

Penny nodded, trying not to think about what their giving up meant. "I'd better go. I can slip back into fifth period class if I hurry."

"Want me to walk over with you?"

"Good grief, no! That would be all over Wayne County by nightfall."

"Yeah. Well, I'm not going back right away. Think I'll hang out here for a while. Thanks for coming, Penny. I'll give you a ring tonight."

"Sure." Penny let herself out and made her way back to school. She slipped in a side door and joined her classmates as they came out of gym class. She might as well have gone home because she remembered nothing taught for the remainder of the day.

Chris phoned that night to report he was grounded. "Mr. Rodenberry saw me sneak out of school and called Mom this evening. She was really steamed! I can't go anywhere except school for a whole week."

Penny tried to lighten the situation. "Guess we'll have to eat all Aunt Martha's cookies ourselves."

"Low blow, Penny," Chris said, groaning.

"I'll save some for you."

"Those cookies will grow mold after Mom sees that phone bill. She'll really go ballistic then," Chris said mournfully.

"Did your mom get the job?"

"Yeah. She was real happy, until she got my bad news. Now she's disappointed in me. What about you? Did you get caught?"

"No," Penny said, feeling guilty. Suddenly she was alarmed. "You aren't moving to Roanoke, are you?"

"No way. You're stuck with ole unreliable, untrustworthy me."

"I'll try to bear up," she replied. "We all have burdens to carry."

"Jeez, thanks! You sure know how to make a guy feel good."

Penny heard a muffled snicker on the line. "Guess we'd better hang up, Chris. Somebody needs to blow her nose."

Chris chuckled. "I hope our friend doesn't have a cold."

"Nosiness isn't catching," Penny assured him. A loud click sounded on the line. "Night, Chris."

For the next two days Penny got up, dressed, ate, and went to school like a robot. Time was passing. All Hallows' eve was drawing closer. She would sit in class, wondering who would be the next victim. Someone she knew? The thought would send shivers racing through her; otherwise she simply sat and stared off into space.

By Friday afternoon she was a nervous wreck, jumping at every slammed door or dropped book. Three days with very little sleep and very little food had taken a toll. When the last bell rang, Penny came out of her trance and began gathering her books.

"May I see you for a moment, Penny?"

The voice coming from behind her startled her so badly she dropped everything on the floor.

"Here, let me help," Miss Longacre said. "I'm sorry I startled you." She began gathering the scattered papers. "I couldn't help noticing that something has been bothering you these last few days. Can I help?"

"No, ma'am." Penny picked up some papers and dropped others. "I—I think I have the flu."

Miss Longacre didn't seem to hear the lie. She was thumbing through a batch of Penny's sketches. "Are these your work, Penny?"

"Just some old pen and ink drawings," Penny said with a shrug.

"They're wonderful! Where did you study?"

Penny gave the teacher a puzzled look. "I study at home."

Miss Longacre's eyes crinkled with laughter. "No, I meant where did you study art. Who taught you?"

"Nobody. I just draw and paint to please myself," Penny said, retrieving the sketches.

"Oh, my! I'm impressed. You're wasting your time in this school. You should be in a school for the arts."

Penny felt a glow of pleasure before she came back to earth. "Thanks. But no school would take a student like me. Real artists aren't dyslexic."

"That isn't true! Haven't you heard of Patricia Buckley Moss? She a wonderful artist and she is dyslexic. She exhibits all over the world, even has a gallery not far from here."

"I'm sure she's wonderful," Penny said, shaking her head. "But my art is just a hobby. School wouldn't help me."

"Of course it would! Learning about other artists and their techniques would be very beneficial to you. Haven't you ever had a painting that wouldn't come out the way you wanted? Some scene you couldn't quite capture?"

Like the curtain going up at a school play, the shadows in Penny's mind suddenly lifted. She saw what had been hiding from her!

The massive, solitary oak with its perfect shape and

crown of mistletoe dominated the narrow little valley. Enormous power and evil flowed from it.

Penny gasped.

"What's wrong?" Miss Longacre asked, reaching out to steady Penny.

"Nothing." The shadows closed in again, hiding the tree.

"May I keep some of these? I'd like to show them to a friend who—"

Penny thrust the rest of the drawings into the teacher's outstretched hand and fled.

A coppery taste of fear filled her mouth as she raced toward the town square. It knows I know, it knows I know echoed in her head and gave wings to her feet. She was totally unaware of the curious stares and honking horns.

She had to find Chris! It wasn't too late!

CHAPTER TWELVE

"This isn't your problem!"

"It is! Whether I like it or not, I'm part of this."

Chris towered over her, glaring. "You only got involved because of me. Now tell me where this tree is!"

Penny glared back. "Even with the blue blazes, you couldn't find the glen. You'd be lost in five minutes."

A flush darkened Chris's face. "Okay, so I'm a klutz in the woods. Can't you show me today? I'll get back there tomorrow if I have to drop bread crumbs."

The idea of Chris sprinkling a bread trail made Penny smile.

Seeing this, Chris wheedled, "Come on, Penny. We don't have that much daylight left."

They had been arguing since she'd grabbed him when he got off the school bus fifteen minutes ago. His protective attitude rubbed her the wrong way. Made her forget the terrifying image of that vengeful, all-seeing tree. Luckily, she hadn't told him about that! But he was right about one thing: they didn't have much time. "All right. I guess I could mark the trail for you. Not with bread crumbs though." Reluctantly, she began walking. "What's spooked you, Chris?"

"I've been reading Uncle Pat's books and going through the journals. Some of the things that happened to my ancestors—especially those who came close—were pretty gruesome. This isn't some game. It's dangerous."

"What things are you talking about?"

"One guy died stark-raving mad in an institution. One died after falling into a hole full of rattlesnakes. Two suffered lingering deaths from some kind of mysterious poison. Uncle Pat fell off a cliff."

"But he didn't die from his fall," Penny said thoughtfully. "He, too, died from a poison, didn't he?"

"Yeah. See what I mean? Finding the Druid oak is dangerous. Even Dr. Jones knew that."

Penny was silent for a few minutes, thinking. "Chris, did you read anything about mistletoe?" she asked out of the blue.

"Sure. It was the Druids' sacred plant."

"Yes. They used it in all their ceremonies. It was both life-giving and death-bringing."

"Say what?"

"I read that the Druids used mistletoe as a powerful medicine and also as a potent poison. Do you think your uncle might have been poisoned when it looked as if he might recover?"

Chris chewed on his lower lip. "I never thought of that. It's possible. But that would mean—"

"Your uncle's theory was right," she finished. A cold feeling crept up her back. "There *is* a vate protecting the Druid."

They had reached Deadman's Curve only a few yards from the blue-blazed trail on Little Bear. Chris stopped abruptly and turned to look at her with horror on his face. "That does it! You're not going any farther. I'll find that cursed tree on my own."

102

"You can't stop—"

Chris lunged at her, knocking her backward over the steel guardrail. He landed on top of her and rolled away. A topsy-turvy world of sky, rocks, and trees sped by her. Confusing sounds of mashing metal, shrieking sirens, and shouting sounded in her ears. Then all motion and sound ceased and she floated in a silent blackness....

"Steady. Easy does it. There ya go."

Hands poked and pried at her body. Her head hurt. Head? She hurt all over!

"She's comin' around."

Penny forced her eyes open. Brushing away the offending hands, she tried to sit up. "What ..."

Sheriff Peale's face swam into her view. He gently pushed her down. "Hold still. Let the medic do his job. You had a nasty fall."

That she remembered! Everything else was a blur. "Chris?"

"He's being taken care of. You're lucky he has good reflexes. Preacher Cawper almost ran you over with that fancy car of his."

"Ready, Sheriff."

"Take her away. I'll be down in a few minutes."

Penny was lifted into an ambulance and whisked away. In spite of the wild ride, she closed her eyes and tried to make sense out of what had happened. Thinking was difficult.... The next thing she knew, she was lying on a table with Dr. Burton's nurse looking down at her. "Miss Ada? What happened?"

"Now, don't you fret," the round-faced, kindly nurse said. "You're just scraped and bruised a little. I'm cleaning you up a bit while Doctor sets the Williams boy's arm."

Penny ignored the sting of the antiseptic. "Chris broke his arm?"

Miss Ada's starched white cap bobbed. "It's not a bad break. Hunter Bell and the sheriff witnessed the whole thing. Preacher's car missed you two by inches. That crazy fool never even tried to brake! There. That does it. Doctor will be here shortly to check on that bump on your noggin."

"Don't go. Keep me company," Penny begged, sitting up. Her head felt as if a herd of horses were stampeding through it. "What happened to Preacher Cawper?"

"Went to the bottom with his car. Right through the guardrail. He's deader than yesterday's ashes."

Penny shuddered. "How awful."

Miss Ada patted her knee. "Don't worry your head about that one. Sheriff Peale thinks he tried to kill you and I bet he's right. I always said he was no good, that Preacher Cawper."

"Why? He seemed nice enough to me."

The clinic nurse shook her head disdainfully. "I know. Butter wouldn't melt in that preacher's mouth when you talked with him. But I saw how he treated his wife! He wanted a son in the worst way, and when that poor little thing miscarried, he was furious. Ranted and raved so's the whole place could hear. Told her she was worthless. If Doctor hadn't been there, he'd have hit her. Now, I ask you, is that any way for a Christian to act?"

"No, ma'am."

Nodding, Miss Ada said, "I told Doctor afterward that a man with a temper like that was dangerous. What do you suppose set him off this time?"

"I have no idea," Penny said. But she did. The pieces of the puzzle fell into place. The Druid had called his vate to protect him. Preacher Cawper had to be the vate. In trying to kill them before they reached the tree, the vate had given away his identity. Who would have ever suspected a minister? Another thought occurred to her and she gasped aloud. No wonder he wanted a son—to carry on the family task as a vate.

Nurse Ada was beside her in a flash. "Are you hurting more?"

"No, I just moved my head too fast. Can I see Chris? It's important."

"You can do that in just a moment," Dr. Burton assured her, coming through a side door. "The EMT says you're only bruised up a bit, but I'll check to make certain. Martha and Jake are on their way."

"You didn't need to call them! How's Chris?"

The burly, bearlike doctor laughed. "Jake would have had my head for breakfast if I hadn't called him. Young Mr. Williams is fine, except for a few bruises and a broken left arm. You are both very lucky from what I gathered. You may not feel lucky by tomorrow morning though. You're going to feel as if you've been kicked by a Missouri mule."

"Can I see him?"

The doctor had finished his gentle inspection. "He's waiting for you in the other room. Rather anxiously, I might add."

Penny slipped off the table and stood on wobbly legs. "Thanks, Dr. Burton."

The doctor winked. "Go through that door, Penny. The sheriff's waiting in the hall. I'll stall him and give you a few minutes alone."

Penny gave his arm a grateful squeeze. "Thanks."

"I remember what it was like to be young."

Miss Ada snorted.

Penny hurried into the adjoining room. She could hardly

wait to tell Chris the news. But when she saw him all other matters flew straight out of her head. He was so pale! His eyes—usually a bright, lively blue—were cloudy and dulled by pain.

Chris held out his good arm. "Are you really okay?"

"Yes," she answered, moving toward him. She lightly touched his cast. "Does it hurt much?"

"Nah. Doc gave me something before he set it. Did they tell you why I tackled you?"

"They said Pastor Cawper lost control of his car."

"Lost control? Jeez, Louise! The guy meant to kill us! I'll never forget that face. The question is why?"

Before she could reply, Sheriff Peale burst into the room. "Doc says you're able to answer a few questions now. Let's hear your version of what happened. You first, Penny. Start at the beginning."

For a moment her thoughts spun wildly. What should she say? Should she tell the sheriff what she knew? Would he believe such a wild tale. Would anybody? Or would they shut her up in a mental institution? She focused on Sheriff Peale's stern face and answered calmly. "I had some good news to share with Chris. Then we decided to go for a hike. We were walking and talking when he suddenly tackled me and I went down the mountain. You know the rest."

Sheriff Peale's eyes swung toward Chris. "Is that correct?"

"That's it. I happened to look up and saw this car headed straight for us. I knocked Penny down. I didn't have time to think about it."

"There were no skid marks," the sheriff said, watching them carefully. "Either of you know why the preacher would want to kill you?"

Penny and Chris shook their heads.

"It doesn't make sense," Chris said. "I didn't even know the man."

The sheriff fixed Penny with a flinty stare. "I suppose you have no idea why this Cawper was following you, even keeping an eye on your place?"

"No, sir. Was he?" Penny said, trying to control a burst of fear that tingled every nerve in her body.

Sheriff Peale's eyes bored into her. "He was. Remember when I told you I was going to keep an eye on you? Well, I did. And somehow this preacher was always in the vicinity, too. Always had a reason, you understand. But it made me suspicious. So I ran a little background check on the man. Guess what I found?"

"I—I don't know."

"Seems this Pastor John Cawper—or Cooper, as he sometimes called himself—had lived in several areas where girls had gone missing. What do you make of that?"

She refused to meet the sheriff's eyes. "Preachers move around all the time."

"Come on, Penny," the sheriff ordered. "What do you know that made this man try to kill you? And your friend, too. What did you see up on Big Bear? It must have been something that connected him with Melissa's death. Think, girl!"

Chris came to her rescue. "The man was crazy! I'll never forget that maniac's face."

"Sure he was crazy," Sheriff Peale snapped. "You'd have to be crazy to kill girls like that. What I want is proof. I don't have a shred of evidence to prove my theory. Help me out here, Penny."

She shot a look at Chris's face and saw comprehension dawn. He knew Cawper was the vate! Shrugging helplessly, she said, "I'd like to help you, but I don't know anything. I can't help it if you or Preacher Cawper thought I did."

Sheriff Peale glared at both of them. "He wouldn't try to kill you without a reason."

Neither Chris nor Penny said a word.

"All right. The man's dead. Right now I can't prove he had anything at all to do with those missing or dead girls. But I think you can be sure there'll be no more." Turning crisply on his heels, he marched out, leaving the door open behind him.

Penny and Chris looked at each other with a growing sense of horror. They knew the sheriff was wrong. The vate was dead but the Druid curse was not broken.

Chris slid off the table and awkwardly removed the stone cross from around his neck. With shaky fingers, he placed it over her head.

"Why . . . ?"

"Please. I'll feel better."

"But . . ."

"Tomorrow's our last chance," he whispered, as hurrying feet approached. "Wait for my call. Promise?"

"Promise," Penny said as Martha, Jake, and Mrs. Williams came in and smothered them with hugs, kisses, and questions.

CHAPTER THIRTEEN

The phone rang off the hook all morning. None of the calls was from Chris.

Penny wandered restlessly through the house, letting her aunt answer the phone and the questions. She'd had a night full of horrible dreams. Her body felt as if six Missouri mules had taken turns kicking it. She was worried about Chris. And time was slipping away toward All Hallows' eve.

When one o'clock came and Chris still hadn't made contact, she phoned him.

Mrs. Williams answered on the first ring. "Penny, I'm so glad you called. Chris tried to get through this morning. How are you?"

"I'm okay. How's Chris?"

"Asleep," Mrs. Williams answered with a nervous giggle. "He was so restless last night and his arm was hurting. But he wouldn't take the medication Dr. Burton prescribed. So I slipped some into his morning snack. It worked. It knocked him right out."

"Oh, no!"

"I'll tell him you called and are all right. With a few hours of rest, he'll feel much better."

"I'm sure he will," Penny managed to say after swallowing around the lump in her throat.

"Get some rest yourself. You sound very upset."

"I will. Tell Chris I called . . . and not to worry. I'll take care of—uh—everything. Please, don't forget, Mrs. Williams."

"I'll deliver your message word for word," promised Mrs. Williams.

Penny put down the phone, shaking her head in amazement. What made her say that? Who did she think she was? Joan of Arc? Wonder Woman? No way! She was a solitary. Someone who minded her own business. And this was certainly was *not* her business. Jeez, she wasn't even a Moore!

She dragged her tired body upstairs and sprawled across her bed. A long nap would make her feel better. "Why should I care what happens tonight?" she muttered, clutching her one-eyed bear. "*I* won't be out running around. I know better."

Her selfish words echoed in her head. Penny's eyes flew open. What was the matter with her? She couldn't allow another girl to be sacrificed. Not when she knew how to stop the slaughter. Quickly, she slid off the bed, washed her face in cold water, and began packing her backpack. Doubt dogged her every move. Fear fumbled her fingers. Nevertheless, she kept going.

Martha was on the phone again when she tiptoed downstairs. She went to the kitchen, left a note, gathered a few supplies, and slipped out the back door. Collecting Rusty, she set off through the orchard.

Rusty smelled her fear and stuck close by her side. His big, dark eyes questioned her.

"It's okay, boy," she said, pausing to cut off a staff of mountain ash. Her hands shook even as the calm words came out. "If not me, then who? Chris is out of it. Nobody else is gonna believe this wild tale. That just leaves you and me. We'll be okay. The vate's dead and the Druid oak can't do anything until dusk. We have lots of time."

Head tilted to one side, Rusty listened as if he understood every word. He gave her hand a comforting lick, but he didn't look convinced.

Getting to Little Bear without being seen took twice as long as usual. Especially since her sneakers felt like lead boots. She was trembling with fatigue by the time she found the glen. "So far, so good," she whispered, standing on the same overhanging rock.

The scene hadn't changed, except the trees were bare. It made the fluffy ring of mistletoe more visible. All looked peaceful in the secluded, narrow valley.

"Let's go down, boy."

Rusty crouched on his belly with his ears laid back and whined.

"Oh, come on. This bank isn't so steep." To show him, she began scrambling down the slope.

Reluctantly, Rusty followed.

From ground level, the oak was even more impressive. It rose some eighty feet into the air with its massive trunk supporting limbs as large as some trees. The ground under the tree was barren. No grass. No leaves. No acorns.

"So what?" Penny said, looking at the tree defiantly. "If you are just an ordinary, three-hundred-year-old oak, this won't amount to a hill of beans. I'll be the one who feels foolish. But, if you really are the spirit of that Druid priest, I know how to stop you." She dropped her backpack a few yards from the tree. "Sit. Stay," she ordered Rusty. Then, ash stick in hand, she marched toward the tree.

Rusty sat by her backpack, following her progress with his eyes and whimpering.

"Hush!" Penny commanded as anger surged through her. "I feel stupid enough without your comments. I don't believe in evil spirits. I bet Chris is sitting in his nice, warm bed laughing his head off."

When the circle was complete she stepped back, replaying Dr. Jones's strange chant in her mind. The words came back in perfect rhythm. Once again she was grateful for her excellent recall. She started forward. *"Athair—"*

Rusty grabbed her sweatshirt and dragged her backward.

Penny slapped his muzzle furiously. "Let go of me, you yellow-bellied coward! Get outta here! Go home! You're no help at all."

Ears and tail down, Rusty backed a few feet away.

"Home!" It took several yells and a rock flung at him, but Rusty finally ran off.

"Stupid dog! Now, where was I?" It took several minutes for her to collect herself and begin again. Concentrating with all her might, she walked the circle chanting, *"Athair, Oregetoria, Catumoros! Arglwydd orwai trawy'r anialwch. Sygn traws.* Amen."

After she'd completed the prescribed three circuits she felt as if she'd walked ten miles. Exhausted, she sat down, unpacked her backpack, and waited for something to happen.

Nothing did.

The air was perfectly still. No leaves rustled. No bird sang. No forest creatures scuttled through the underbrush to break the silence.

Penny felt utterly alone ... abandoned. She wished she hadn't sent Rusty away. Why had she? She couldn't remember what he'd done, though she did recall throwing a rock. At Rusty? Her face burned. Yes! She'd rocked him. Ordered him home.

As she looked at the huge oak with its bare branches etched against the evening sky, the consequences of her action hit her. Rusty always obeyed. He would go home without her and Aunt Martha and Uncle Jake would be frantic. They'd think something awful had happened. Yesterday had been bad enough. She couldn't let them worry again! Panicked, she began to gather her things. If she hurried, she could get home before they missed her. . . .

A glowing heat radiated on her chest. Penny yanked the stone cross from beneath her heavy sweatshirt. The smooth stone felt warm and comforting. Holding it in her palm calmed her. The last instruction from Dr. Jones echoed in her head: " 'Stay and watch until the spell be broken.' " No matter what happened, she *must* stay! Penny gathered her courage and settled back to watch and wait.

Darkness comes quickly in the mountains. The sun sets behind the hills, and after a few minutes of twilight, an inky blackness settles over the earth until moonrise.

Until the light faded, Penny sketched. Then she entertained herself by softly singing every song she knew: hymns, popular, and country. She was tempted to light the dark with the flashlight she'd grabbed in the kitchen, but she wasn't sure how strong the batteries were. Occasionally, she used the flash to check on the Druid oak. Nothing ever changed. Minutes ticked by like hours. Her eyes felt as heavy and droopy as a fully laden apple tree. If only she could rest them for a few—

"Penny! Help! I'm hurt!"

Her eyes flew open. She turned on the flashlight and played it around. "Chris?"

"Over here. Hurry!"

She turned the beam toward the voice. On a bank behind the oak she could dimly see Chris sprawled on a pile of rocks. His leg was bent underneath him at an odd angle. . . . "Hold on! I'm coming!" Jumping up, she started forward. Something twinned around her ankle and she fell flat. Frantically, she picked at the tangled straps of her backpack.

Inches from the line drawn around the tree, the flashlight shone on the spot where Chris had moaned in agony.

Penny gave her attention to the knots which seemed to have a clinging life of their own. When she was finally loose, she looked up. For a full moment her heart seemed to stop beating. There was no Chris! The weak ray of light revealed only an outcrop of rocks. Had she dreamed him? NO! She'd seen him. Heard him. Where was he? Now her heart thumped madly, making up for lost time. With shaky fingers, she reached for the flashlight.

The line drawn in the dirt stood out like a ravine. Penny gasped. The circle! She'd almost broken the holy circle! Allowed the Druid to escape.

Anger coursed through her as she realized what had happened. The Druid oak might be motionless, but it was not powerless. Penny shook her fist at the tree. "You tried to trick me! Well, it won't work. I'm keeping watch until you are destroyed!"

A wave of hate slammed into her like a giant fist. The bare branches of the oak writhed like masses of huge snakes. They reached for her. . . .

Penny scooched backward. The limbs and the fury could not pass the holy circle. She turned off the flash and remained motionless until her breathing slowed. "Don't let me fail," she prayed softly. "Too many girls have died. Give me strength to stay here until it's over."

A sliver of moon rose in the night sky, shedding an eerie light over the little valley. Somehow that meager light was a comfort. Senses alert, she settled back to await the dawn.

Sometime later her straining ears picked up a sound. Something was moving on the bank behind her. Turning swiftly, she saw a pair of red eyes gleaming at her in the dark. Fear shot through her. Wolf? Cougar? Another trick? Just as she turned the flashlight upwards, the eyes disappeared. "Probably only a raccoon," she muttered and turned back toward the tree.

"Penny! Penny, where are you?"

She let out a mocking laugh. "Fool me once, shame on you. Fool me twice, shame on me. I'm not falling for that ole trick again."

The words had hardly left her mouth when something came crashing out of the underbrush straight for her. Penny turned and flicked her light on. "Go away!"

A dirty, bedraggled Chris and a panting Rusty froze like startled deer in the beam of light.

"Penny? It's me."

"Chris?"

Rusty didn't wait. Tail down, he crept toward her. His eyes begged forgiveness.

Penny reached out and touched real fur. "Oh, Rusty, it really is you," she said, throwing her arms around the quivering dog.

"What about me? Can you shine the light this way? I can't see squat."

"Be careful!" she shouted in sudden alarm. "Stay where you are." She picked up the discarded flash and shone it on the real Chris. Pain and concern played on his face as he hobbled toward her.

"Thank God, you're okay," he said. "I thought for sure the Druid had gotten to you." He sank down beside her.

"I got to him first." She turned the light toward the gigantic tree. "Father Stephen's spell is working."

"Jeez, Louise! How? I have the tape right here in my pocket."

"I remembered it—word for word."

"All that jabberwocky? Get real!"

"It is real," Penny said quietly. "That's the way I learn, Chris. I can remember pages and pages of stuff I hear, if I concentrate. The chant was easy. Staying here alone, guarding against sneaky tricks has been the hard part."

"What sneaky tricks?"

In a calm voice, she told him all that had happened. "We have to be very careful, Chris," she finished.

"We will be," he said grimly. "God knows, I'm sorry you had to do this alone."

"How did you find me? I thought your mom drugged you."

"She did. I was out like a light. When I woke up and looked at the clock I panicked. I grabbed the tape and my Walkman and ran downstairs to call you. Mom gave me your message and that blew my mind."

"Why?"

"Don't play dumb. I knew right away what you were up to," Chris said. "Anyway, I took off with Mom yelling at the top of her lungs. I found the trail with no problem. But that's where the fun began."

"Fun?"

"Yeah. I don't know what happened. I followed the blue blazes—just like you told me—but the trail and the blazes just vanished. I was standing in the middle of nowhere, without a clue about which way to go. It was like a giant maze, Penny. I was sweating bullets. I've been wandering around calling for you since about five o'clock. I really messed up."

Penny flicked her light on the Druid oak. "I think something else might have been at work, Chris."

"You mean the tree?"

"It's very powerful, Chris. It may not be able to move

but it sure can play games with your head. How did you find me?"

"Rusty. I was wandering around like a blind man when he came trotting out of the bushes. I told him 'Find Penny' and he led me here."

"But I sent him home! He always obeys me."

"He didn't this time, thank God. I never would have gotten here on my own."

Huddled together for warmth, the three of them waited and watched. Chris and Penny kept alert by talking about everything from apples to zoology. Toward first light a heavy fog rolled in, draping everything with a thick white curtain.

"I can't see a thing through this stuff," Chris complained.

"It's almost dawn," Penny whispered through a scratchy throat.

As she spoke, the ground began to tremble and shake. A loud whooshing noise and a clap of thunder filled their ears and sent their hearts pounding.

"Let's get outta here!" Chris yelled.

"*No!* It's trying to escape." She clutched Chris and Rusty as they all tumbled backward.

The earth shook and wild streaks of lightning flashed all around them.

Chris yelped in pain.

"What's wrong?"

"Hit my cast," Chris said, gasping. "Phew! What's that smell?"

As quickly as it had begun, the commotion ceased. The air was filled with a gagging stench.

"Rotten eggs," Penny said, trying not to breathe through her nose. Uncle Arly's brimstone came briefly to mind as she peered through the mist. "Look!"

Chris sat up. "The fog's lifting. Hey! The circle's empty. The Druid oak's gone."

"Not quite. Look in the center."

Where once the huge tree had stood there was only a smoldering stump. And, as they watched, that, too, crumbled to black, greasy ashes. A light breeze sprang up, blowing away the awful stench.

"Jeez!"

"We did it," Penny whispered. "No more girls will be sacrificed."

"I hope Uncle Pat knows, wherever he is."

Penny looked down at the stone cross resting on her shirt. It seemed to glow with a special light and warmth. "He does," she said confidently. "I think he and Father Stephen have been with us all night. Now they can rest in peace."

"You felt it, too? I thought I was the only crazy one."

"No. We were not alone," she said, turning to find Chris gazing at her with an expression she'd never seen before. She felt the blood rise in her face and an unaccustomed warmth glowing inside her.

Chris grabbed her in a bear hug. "We really did it!"

A smile tilted her lips and danced in her eyes as she looked up at Chris. "Yes, we did. Guess I worked myself right out of a job. You won't need me anymore."

"Hey, you can't get rid of me that easily. I need you. I'm still a greenhorn."

Overhead a bird greeted the new day with joyous song. It mirrored the song in Penny's heart. Her mountains were free once more, and she had found another place where she belonged.

From out of the Shadows...
Stories Filled With Mystery and Suspense by
MARY DOWNING HAHN

THE TIME OF THE WITCH
71116-8/ $3.99 US/ $4.99 Can

It is the middle of the night and suddenly Laura is awake, trembling with fear. Just beneath her bedroom window, a strange-looking old woman is standing in the moonlight—staring at Laura.

STEPPING ON THE CRACKS
71900-2/ $3.99 US/ $4.99 Can

THE DEAD MAN IN INDIAN CREEK
71362-4/ $3.50 US/ $4.25 Can

THE DOLL IN THE GARDEN
70865-5/ $3.50 US/ $4.25 Can

FOLLOWING THE MYSTERY MAN
70677-6/ $3.99 US/ $4.99 Can

TALLAHASSEE HIGGINS
70500-1/ $3.50 US/ $4.25 Can

WAIT TILL HELEN COMES
70442-0/ $3.50 US/ $4.25 Can

THE SPANISH KIDNAPPING DISASTER
71712-3/ $3.50 US/ $4.25 Can

Buy these books at your local bookstore or use this coupon for ordering:

Mail to: Avon Books, Dept BP, Box 767, Rte 2, Dresden, TN 38225   C
Please send me the book(s) I have checked above.
❏ My check or money order— no cash or CODs please— for $_____is enclosed
(please add $1.50 to cover postage and handling for each book ordered— Canadian residents add 7% GST).
❏ Charge my VISA/MC Acct#_____Exp Date_____
Minimum credit card order is two books or $6.00 (please add postage and handling charge of $1.50 per book — Canadian residents add 7% GST). For faster service, call 1-800-762-0779. Residents of Tennessee, please call 1-800-633-1607. Prices and numbers are subject to change without notice. Please allow six to eight weeks for delivery.

Name_____
Address_____
City_____State/Zip_____
Telephone No._____   MDH 0194

THE MAGIC CONTINUES...
WITH
LYNNE REID BANKS

THE MYSTERY OF THE CUPBOARD
72013-2/$3.99 US/$4.99 Can

THE SECRET OF THE INDIAN
71040-4/$3.99 US

THE INDIAN IN THE CUPBOARD
60012-9/$3.99 US/$4.99 Can

THE RETURN OF THE INDIAN
70284-3/$3.99 US

I, HOUDINI
70649-0/$3.99 US

THE FAIRY REBEL
70650-4/$3.99 US

THE FARTHEST-AWAY MOUNTAIN
71303-9/$3.99 US

ONE MORE RIVER
71563-5/$3.99 US

THE ADVENTURES OF KING MIDAS
71564-3/$3.99 US

Buy these books at your local bookstore or use this coupon for ordering:

Mail to: Avon Books, Dept BP, Box 767, Rte 2, Dresden, TN 38225   C
Please send me the book(s) I have checked above.
❏ My check or money order— no cash or CODs please— for $_____ is enclosed
(please add $1.50 to cover postage and handling for each book ordered— Canadian residents add 7% GST).
❏ Charge my VISA/MC Acct#_____ Exp Date_____
Minimum credit card order is two books or $6.00 (please add postage and handling charge of $1.50 per book — Canadian residents add 7% GST). For faster service, call 1-800-762-0779. Residents of Tennessee, please call 1-800-633-1607. Prices and numbers are subject to change without notice. Please allow six to eight weeks for delivery.

Name_____
Address_____
City_____State/Zip_____
Telephone No._____

LRB 0694